Honorable
Armed Forces of the United States of America

This is to certify that
Captain Sam Cade
is hereby honorably discharged from the
United States Air Force due to medical reasons
and expiration of the term of service
(thereby allowing him to reunite with his
soon-to-be ex-wife).
This certificate is awarded as testimonial of
Honest and Faithful Service.

Harlequin American Romance presents
MILLIONAIRE, MONTANA, where twelve lucky souls have
won a multimillion-dollar jackpot.

Dear Reader,

Our yearlong twentieth-anniversary celebration continues with a spectacular lineup, starting with *Saved by a Texas-Sized Wedding*, beloved author Judy Christenberry's 50th book. Don't miss this delightful addition to the popular series TOTS FOR TEXANS. It's a marriage-of-convenience story that will warm your heart!

Priceless Marriage by Bonnie Gardner is the latest installment in the MILLIONAIRE, MONTANA continuity series, in which a "Main Street Millionaire" claims her "ex" as her own. Jacqueline Diamond pens another charming story in THE BABIES OF DOCTORS CIRCLE series with *Prescription: Marry Her Immediately*. Here a confirmed bachelor doctor enlists the help of his gorgeous best friend in order to win custody of his orphaned niece and nephew. And let us welcome a new author to the Harlequin American Romance family. Kaitlyn Rice makes her sparkling debut with *Ten Acres and Twins*.

It's an exciting year for Harlequin American Romance, and we invite you to join the celebration this month and far into the future!

Melissa Jeglinski
Associate Senior Editor
Harlequin American Romance

PRICELESS MARRIAGE
Bonnie Gardner

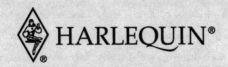

HARLEQUIN®

TORONTO • NEW YORK • LONDON
AMSTERDAM • PARIS • SYDNEY • HAMBURG
STOCKHOLM • ATHENS • TOKYO • MILAN • MADRID
PRAGUE • WARSAW • BUDAPEST • AUCKLAND

To Mud, as always.

To Paige for having faith in me when
I wasn't sure I did. Thanks a bunch.

Special thanks and acknowledgment are given to
Bonnie Gardner for her contribution to the
MILLIONAIRE, MONTANA series.

ISBN 0-373-16970-1

PRICELESS MARRIAGE

Copyright © 2003 by Harlequin Books S.A.

Visit us at www.eHarlequin.com

Printed in U.S.A.

ABOUT THE AUTHOR

Bonnie Gardner has finally figured out what she wants to do when she grows up. After a varied career that included such jobs as switchboard operator, draftsman and exercise instructor, she went back to college and became an English teacher. As a teacher, she took a course on how to teach writing to high school students and caught the bug herself.

She lives in northern Alabama with her husband of over thirty years, her own military hero. After following him around from air force base to air force base, she has finally gotten to settle down. They have two grown sons, one of whom is now serving in the air force. She loves to read, cook, garden and, of course, write.

She would love to hear from her readers. You can write to her at P.O. Box 442, Meridianville, AL 35759.

Books by Bonnie Gardner

HARLEQUIN AMERICAN ROMANCE

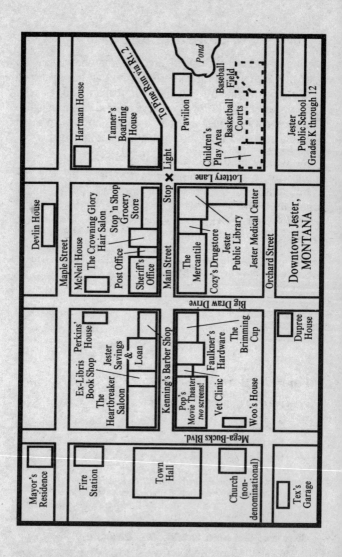

Prologue

Trembling with excitement, Ruby Cade stumbled back into the Mercantile, the closest thing to a department store in hardscrabble Jester, Montana. She turned the sign to Closed, then locked the door behind her. Whether she was shivering from the bitter January cold or the startling, wonderful, absolutely fantastic news she'd just received, Ruby didn't know, and she didn't really care. All she knew was that she couldn't contain her excitement anymore. She had to share the news with her husband, Sam.

Right away.

Now.

The unbelievable had happened!

She'd won! They'd won!

One of the Big Draw lottery tickets that she and her friends purchased every week had actually won!

They were rich. No, more than rich.

They were millionaires!

The twelve of them would split forty million dollars! Ruby was too excited to do the math about what the total would be after taxes, but whatever their share was, she and Sam would be millionaires!

As she rummaged frantically though the cubbyholes of the ancient rolltop desk in the store office, her mind reeled with the implications of what this unexpected infusion of money would do for the town of Jester, which had been barely holding on during the recent economic downturn. Finally, Ruby located the emergency contact number that Sam had left her.

Sam was an elite Air Force Special Operations combat controller who was currently stationed overseas, close to one of the dangerous hot spots in the Middle East. Usually, she waited for Sam to call her from his overseas military base for their twice-weekly chats, but this news was too spectacular to put off until Saturday. Sam had left the number in case of an emergency. Her good news wasn't an emergency, but it certainly was urgent.

Sam was going to flip! Their whole life was going to change, Ruby couldn't help thinking.

As she dialed in the endless string of digits to connect with the base where Sam was stationed, Ruby hoped that this would be the news that would finally bring her husband home. For good.

Brimming with excitement, she listened impatiently as the phone on the other end seemed to ring forever.

Finally, someone answered. Sam's commanding officer, she realized.

Ruby drew a deep breath, swallowed and managed to steady her nerves in order to speak around the enormous lump in her throat. "This is Ruby Cade. May I speak to C-Captain Sam Cade, p-please," she stammered, hoping that Sam would be nearby and available to take the call.

Excitement turned to shock. The answer the faceless voice on the other end of the line gave her was not the one Ruby had expected or wanted. Sam was

not at the base at this time, the officer said. He had
volunteered for a mission, the nature of which the
man could not divulge. He wasn't expected back at
headquarters for several days.

"No!" Ruby gasped. It couldn't be. Not again!
Sam had promised not to volunteer to go into danger
again. He had sworn he wouldn't leave her alone at
home, worrying, anymore.

Her body went weak with the impact of Sam's lie,
and the phone fell out of her nerveless hand to the
cluttered desk.

"Mrs. Cade, do you want to leave a message?" the
tinny, faraway voice asked.

Ruby picked the receiver up again, holding it gingerly as if it were hot. "No. No message," she mumbled. Then she carefully placed the receiver back on
the hook and sank into the swivel chair.

Shock and fear for Sam were quickly replaced by
anger at his duplicity. *He can't do this to me,* Ruby
railed inwardly. He had promised. With the world in
chaos, he had sworn that he would leave the dangerous missions to the younger men and that he would
stay safely behind the lines.

If Sam valued the excitement and danger of his
career in air force combat control more than he did
his wife or their marriage, then so be it, Ruby thought.
She wasn't going to waste her life listening to empty
promises or waiting around for him to come home to
her anymore.

This was the last straw. She was tired of playing
second fiddle to Sam's career. He could have all the
freedom he wanted. She was done.

With the lottery winnings, she was now a woman
of independent means, Ruby realized. She didn't need

Sam, no matter how much she loved him. She'd spent most of their ten-year marriage worrying and waiting at home while he'd gone gallivanting around the world into all sorts of dangerous situations, some so top secret he wouldn't even talk about them. She had hoped that her good news would be the one thing that would finally allow him to leave his dangerous job and start to build a real life with her.

But now all that had changed. He had lied.

He had broken the one promise that had kept her hanging on until now.

She couldn't take the worrying and the waiting anymore. She wouldn't take it.

If Sam wanted to live his life without regard for her needs and feelings, that was fine. But she wasn't going to stand helplessly by and watch. First thing in the morning, she decided, she was going to file for divorce.

Then Ruby crossed her arms over the clutter on the desk, rested her head on them and cried.

Chapter One

Sam Cade gritted his teeth as he bumped along the rutted farm road, that was undoubtedly doing a number on the suspension of the Corvette, until he finally spotted the house that his soon-to-be ex-wife Ruby had purchased after she'd decided to end their marriage. Why she wanted to end the marriage, or buy the farm, he didn't know. But he damned sure intended to find out. Today.

He'd heard that the old Tanner hog farm that she'd bought was a ramshackle mess. From what he could see, the intelligence he'd gathered as he'd quietly nosed around town, hoping to get some insight into what had made Ruby resort to such drastic measures, hadn't been far from wrong.

He chuckled as he thought about his stealth campaign around town. He hadn't spent a lot of time in Jester since he and Ruby had eloped ten years ago, so it was a simple matter to slip into some grubby jeans, not shave, and just lurk around and listen. It was amazing what people talked about when they thought nobody could hear. And he'd heard plenty.

After so many months of anticipating a wonderful, happy homecoming after all his months away, whatever he faced today would be a definite letdown. He drew in a deep breath and pressed on.

Finally, a rambling old ranch-style house came into view, paint peeling and front porch sagging though it proudly held two brand-new wooden porch rockers. He smiled as he noticed the Southern-style porch swing that reminded him of his home in southern Georgia. The house sat on a rise overlooking a field of wildflowers, and it looked like a place Ruby would love. The vista, complete with several cottonwood trees flanking the house, was picturesque, but was the house solid? As Sam drew closer, he could see that the roof had recently been reshingled. Maybe new paint would come next.

Behind the house was a collection of dilapidated sheds and fences, and what appeared to be several new outbuildings. A battered, silver-colored travel trailer the size of a C-130 transport plane was parked behind one of the sheds, flanked by an equally beat-up pickup truck. The only thing that appeared to be new and in one piece was a late-model sport utility vehicle parked in front of the house. Had Ruby spent part of her lottery winnings on that SUV?

The only way to find out was to go in the house and ask. He gunned the engine and surged forward, leaving a cloud of dust behind him.

Sam pulled the dusty silver Corvette up next to the SUV and maneuvered his stiff leg out of the low-slung car. He knew that the Corvette wasn't exactly practical out here in Montana, but until he found out for sure where he stood with Ruby, he would not part with his prized possession which he'd had for years. Well, Ruby had once been his prized possession… Now he wasn't so sure.

Sam had come back to Jester to try to convince Ruby to give him another chance. He truly, honestly loved his wife, and in the past few months he'd had plenty of time to think about where everything had gone wrong. He wanted their marriage to survive. He would do whatever he could to make it work. First he had to convince Ruby to call off the divorce.

And it would really help if he actually knew what had set her mind on ending their marriage. Ruby had always had a temper, but usually she kept it in check. And she was more likely to yell and bluster and quickly get over it than do something as drastic as file for divorce. Usually all it took to distract her was to grab her and kiss her senseless and tumble into bed.

Damn, he wished that would work now, but he was pretty sure it wouldn't. Despite all those lonely nights he'd spent overseas, dreaming of their reunion, and the even lonelier nights in the hospital, he was certain this was not going to be the homecoming he had once envisioned.

Concentrating hard to keep his limp from being noticeable, he strode up the dirt path to the house and onto the porch. Some of the boards had recently been replaced. Evidently, someone was taking care of the place, and Sam was pretty sure Ruby didn't have a clue how to make such repairs it herself. During his undercover investigation around town he'd heard rumors about a stranger helping Ruby out, but nobody knew anything about him. Surely Ruby hadn't turned to another man.

As Sam started to knock on the frame of the screen door, he happened to glance up and catch a glimpse of Ruby through the open window. She was in the arms of a stranger.

Sam stood there for a moment, stunned, and then he lowered his hand and turned. The rumors were right. There *was* another man in his wife's life. *Ex-wife*, he reminded himself. Or soon to be.

Looked like that old board wasn't the only thing that had been replaced.

RUBY LEANED into Nick's embrace. Though she was truly longing for Sam's arms around her, it had been so long since she'd been held by a man, any man, that even Nick's brotherly hug felt good.

"You don't have to thank me, Nick. It's the least I can do. If you can't find someone to finance your venture, you know I'll gladly help out."

Nick stepped back and looked down at Ruby. "Thanks, kiddo. It's enough that you're paying me to help out." He glanced up and let go abruptly. "Uh-oh. You've got company."

Ruby turned quickly, just in time to see the visitor turn away. "Sam," she whispered, her heart skipping a beat. "Shelly O'Rourke said she thought he'd come into the coffee shop the other day, but she hadn't been sure. I didn't believe her."

Then her breath caught. "Oh, my, do you suppose he saw us?" she asked as she hurried to the door.

Nick didn't answer. "I'll just leave you two alone," he said, then disappeared out the back door.

All Ruby could think about, all she could see, was Sam. She threw open the screen door and raced to the top step of the porch. Her heart pounding at his unexpected presence, she called frantically, "Sam! Wait! Don't go."

He looked slowly back over his shoulder, and only then did Ruby notice that he seemed unnaturally pale in the bright May sunlight. He dragged his right leg as if it were too heavy to lift as he trudged toward the Corvette. He'd lost weight, too.

"Please, Sam. Come back!"

He stopped to look at her, his expression unreadable behind aviator-style sunglasses.

"Please, Sam. Don't go," Ruby called after him.

He reached for the car door, then hesitated as if trying to make up his mind. Then he lowered his hand to his side and turned back toward the house. "All right," he said slowly in the deep Georgia drawl that never ceased to make Ruby's insides quiver. He made his way back to her. "I reckon we need to talk."

"Yes, we do," Ruby said breathlessly as he stepped onto the shady porch and removed his glasses. She caught the scent of his aftershave, and that brief whiff of fragrance mixed with the scent that was uniquely Sam made her go all warm and liquid inside, as it always had.

When Sam had gone overseas, Ruby had kept a bottle of that aftershave. It had sat on the bedside table in her room. When she felt particularly lonely and couldn't sleep for missing him, she'd remove the cap and breathe in the scent of the man she loved. Then she'd feel a little less alone. Then, after spending more time with that bottle of aftershave than with the man himself, she'd caught Sam in his lie. In a fit of disgust and anger, she'd emptied the liquid down the toilet and tossed the bottle out, getting a great deal of satisfaction in the thud when it had hit the trash can.

Now all the love—memories of the good times, as

well as the bad—came flooding back to her with one little breath of that fabulous fragrance mixed with the essence of Sam.

She looked up at him. It was hard to tell in the shade of the porch, but he seemed sunken, almost gaunt. Dark circles rimmed his eyes, and even this close his skin looked far too pale in contrast with his dark brown hair, cut military short. And a sprinkling of gray dusted the short hairs at his temples. The gray hair was definitely new.

She wanted to know where he'd been. Why hadn't he gotten in touch with her in the months since she'd filed for divorce? Ruby wanted to know why he'd thrown it all away.

Her heart was pounding. She swallowed, moistened her lips and drew in a deep breath. Then she pulled open the screen door and gestured for Sam to step inside. "Come in," she said, ruing the breathless anticipation he could surely hear in her voice. "We have some catching up to do."

SAM STEPPED INSIDE and waited quietly while his eyes adjusted to the dim interior of the house. He looked around, recognizing the familiar furniture that had traveled with them from one air force base to another, making each house seem like home. Now it was in a home that wasn't his.

"I don't want to intrude," Sam finally said when Ruby didn't volunteer to speak. "You had company."

"Company?" Ruby sounded genuinely puzzled. "Oh. That's just Nick," she said dismissively.

Just Nick? That was rich. Seeing her in that other man's arms had almost cut Sam off at the knees.

He looked at her and she looked back at him as if she were expecting some sort of an explanation. Did he owe her one? Or did she owe *him?* He tried to read the answer in her face, but how could he keep from drowning in her beautiful emerald eyes? "I didn't think this would be so awkward," he finally said.

Ruby shrugged. "You didn't think about a lot of things," she said.

"No, I guess I didn't." But he had. He had lain in his lonely bunk and dreamed of Ruby every night. He had counted the days until he could go home and hold her in his arms forever.

And now, when forever could really happen, Ruby stood in front of him, her arms folded across her chest as though he owed her an explanation. And he didn't know why. He had to understand. He had to get that second chance.

"I'm sorry, Sam," Ruby finally said. "You look tired. Would you like to sit down?"

She took his hand, and that old familiar warmth surged through him as she drew him toward the sofa. Gratefully, Sam sank into the deep cushions. He'd worked like a horse to get his injured leg to hold him up, but it was still weak, and he still wasn't sure it wouldn't give out on him and make him fall on his face in front of Ruby.

Instead of settling down beside him, Ruby took the love seat on the other side of the coffee table. Maybe, for now, that was better. Just looking at her porcelain skin with that golden dusting of freckles had him wanting to touch her, wanting to run his fingers through her fiery hair. But until he was sure his wife wanted him back, he would try to keep his distance.

She crossed her legs demurely at the ankles and rested her hands in her lap, a gesture so familiar, yet strange, considering she was dressed in faded denim jeans and a functional chambray work shirt. Sam thought she looked great in everything, from the tailored business suits she'd worn in California when he'd first met her, to nothing at all. His pulse quickened at the thought.

Damn. He had to get himself together. He swallowed and cleared his throat. "I'm out of the air force," he announced.

Ruby looked up quickly and blinked. Then she blinked again. "You retired? You gave it all up?"

Sam shook his head. "Medical retirement." He nodded in the direction of his right leg. "Can't jump anymore." That was an understatement. The docs had had a hell of a time putting his leg back together, but he wouldn't tell Ruby that right now. He wanted her back on his own terms, not out of pity.

"I'm sorry," she said softly. But was she really? Sam wondered. "I know how much you loved the parachuting and the excitement," she added, closing and opening her hands in her lap. Sam knew that gesture meant she was in turmoil. Did that mean she still cared?

"It was only a job, Ruby, not an emotional commitment," he said, his voice thick with feeling.

She looked at him as if she wasn't sure she'd heard him. "I wish I could believe that."

"You can, Ruby. Have I ever lied to you?"

Suddenly a light seemed to snap on behind Ruby's eyes, and they flashed with anger. "Yes, you have, if you can call a broken promise a lie. Or does it not count if the little wife doesn't know about it? You lied to me, Sam. You broke your promise…and you broke my heart when you did.''

Now Sam thought he understood. All that time, he'd thought that Ruby had filed for divorce because of the money. When he'd tried to return her call five months ago, Honor Lassiter, the other owner of the Mercantile, had breathlessly told him about their lottery win, and at the same time had told him that Ruby wouldn't talk to him.

Weeks later he'd gotten a letter from her Pine Run lawyer. He'd assumed she'd filed because she wanted all the money for herself. Well, that was fine with him. All he wanted was Ruby. She could do whatever she wanted with the money. Except…dump him.

With nothing left to live for, he'd pulled out all the stops and volunteered for every dangerous mission that had come up. His death wish had almost been granted a month later, but when he'd recovered from his injuries, he'd vowed he'd do what he could to get Ruby back. Of course, there'd been no way in hell he was going to crawl back to her. He'd go back to her on his own two feet or not at all. He didn't want her pity. He wanted her.

And he wanted her to want him.

Sam swallowed his pride and drew in a deep breath of air. ''I am truly sorry, Ruby,'' he said. ''I didn't realize then just how strongly you felt about those missions.''

''Why not?'' Ruby challenged. ''A promise is a promise. You can't just back out of one when it's convenient. It should have been very clear how I felt about those missions. We'd been married for almost ten years when I asked you to quit. Surely you could have read the signs.''

"What signs? You never said a word."

"I shouldn't have had to. If you loved me, you should have known."

"Ruby, darlin', I'm not a mind reader. If you didn't like them, if they worried you, you should have told me." Sam thought back to the many times she'd kissed him and smiled bravely as he'd hurried out in the middle of the night. Had it all been an act? A brave front? "Instead, you almost seemed anxious to let me go."

Ruby closed her eyes and leaned back in the love seat. "I didn't want to worry you, Sam. I thought you had enough to contend with without having to worry about me at home. After all, I wasn't going off into harm's way."

"You could have told me that when I came home. I wasn't going to war then," he reminded her gently.

"Then I didn't need to. Then you were there. Then things were right and good. But that still doesn't change the fact that you broke your promise. I never would have agreed to that stupid plan to let you take that last overseas assignment if I'd had any idea you'd put yourself in danger."

Sam smiled. It was true. Being at home was always great, like a honeymoon every day, but they'd never really talked. Not about the important stuff, anyway. "Ruby, at the time I made that promise, I truly meant it. But circumstances changed."

Ruby raised her hands in protest. "Don't give me that," she protested sharply. "You made a promise to me. And you broke it. Just because you didn't expect me to find out doesn't change things. I did find out, Sam. I did. And you...broke my heart."

Hearing her say that again almost broke his, but

Sam pulled himself together. "I would have told you about it, Ruby. When I could."

"Can you tell me now, or is it another one of those if-I-tell-you-I'll-have-to-kill-you things?" she challenged.

A lot of details were still classified, but Sam figured he could tell her some. "Let's just say a teammate needed help and there was no one else available at the time." He could see that Ruby wasn't swallowing it. "I can't tell you any more, Ruby. I would if I could. Just believe me. I would not have gone if there had been anyone else to do it." Ruby knew full well that a combat controller never left a fallen buddy behind. Surely, she understood that.

Ruby started to say something, then snapped her mouth shut. After a long moment's pause, she said carefully, "You've given me a lot to think about, Sam. And I don't want to make a hasty decision this time. Leave me alone and let me think about it."

Sam got to his feet. "Fair enough," he said, restraining himself from cheering. "I know I've got to prove myself to you, and I'll do just that. In the meantime, I'm staying at Gwen Tanner's boardinghouse if you need to reach me." Of course, he'd rather be staying here, but he figured he wouldn't push his luck. Yet. As he took his leave, he just prayed that Ruby would come to the right conclusion.

Chapter Two

Ruby stood in the doorway and watched Sam drive away in that stupid Corvette he loved so much. He'd once told her that driving it was the closest thing to flying that he could do on the ground. Personally, riding in it scared her to death. The sports car looked so out of place on the dirt roads among the rolling hills of eastern Montana. She wondered if Sam would ever give it up.

She was truly glad that he had left the air force. She was glad he'd come to her, but she still wasn't certain that she really came first with him. Yes, his explanation about why he'd gone on that mission sounded good, but was that the whole truth? Would he even have told her that much if he hadn't been caught lying?

If he hadn't injured his leg so that he could no longer do the job, would he have come home now? Would he have made the same decision? And if his leg became stronger, would he just find some other dangerous occupation? She had to know.

She thought she'd much rather hold him at arm's length until she was sure he was going to stay. She couldn't bear to have him break her heart again.

She watched until the car bounced out of sight, then she turned back inside.

Nick was there. When had he come back in?

"So, that was Sam," he said.

"Yes, that was Sam."

"What did he want?"

"Me," Ruby said simply.

"You gonna let him have what he wants?"

Ruby drew in a deep breath. "I don't know, Nick. I truly don't know." And she didn't want to talk to Nick about it. She had to figure this out by herself.

She'd believed she'd thought it all through. She'd figured she'd made the right decision to file for divorce. And once she'd made up her mind, she'd been determined to stick to her decision.

Then she'd seen Sam again. In the flesh, the living breathing man was a lot harder to forget than a box of snapshots and a few memories. Or a bottle of aftershave.

She smiled sadly. "I don't feel much like company right now, Nick," she murmured. "Do you mind?"

Nick just smiled and backed away. "I don't mind, kid. I expect you have some thinking to do. I'll just get my supper in town tonight." He tipped an imaginary hat and left as quietly as he'd come.

Ruby sank to the sofa where Sam had been sitting only a few moments before. Was it her imagination or could she still feel the warmth of his body on the cushions? She picked up one of the throw pillows and hugged it to her breast.

She hadn't anticipated this.

She hadn't expected that Sam would leave the air force now, not after that last—what?—misunderstanding? Or had the air force left him? He had said that he'd been let out on medical retirement. She closed her eyes and tried to push all the worries and doubts out of her mind, but they wouldn't go. Why did it all have to be so complicated?

If Sam hadn't been hurt, would he still have come home to her?

Why couldn't life be simple and happy as it had been when she was a child?

Ruby closed her eyes and heaved a huge sigh. Why couldn't she be certain that Sam loved her for herself, and not just because he could no longer have his first love, or because he wanted to get his hands on all the lottery money? Would she ever know that he loved her more than the air force and the dangerous job he'd done so well?

More than a million dollars?

Did he love her just for herself?

SAM DROVE SLOWLY BACK through the small town of Jester. He'd never understood why Ruby had been so homesick for this tiny piece of real estate out in the middle of nowhere, this one-stoplight town, where winters could be brutal, at least to a guy raised in the Deep South, as he had been. He might have passed winter survival training, but he hadn't liked it.

When he'd met her, Ruby had had a career as a buyer for a large department store near Travis Air Force Base in California, where he'd been stationed at the time. He'd thought she'd enjoyed the pace and the amenities of the large city. It had surprised him enough that she'd wanted to settle for co-owning the Mercantile in Jester, but at least she had the training for it. Now she wanted to farm? He could think of better things to waste a couple million dollars on.

True, she'd always loved making things grow. And, hell, when they'd first met, she'd had more tropical plants in her apartment than the set of a Tarzan movie. And after they'd married, wherever they lived, whether it be in base housing or off base, she'd always had a garden plot. Maybe this wasn't such a far-fetched idea, after all. Ruby certainly had a green thumb.

She had never felt comfortable living in military housing, and she'd never enjoyed the camaraderie he'd felt with his unit. So when he'd been given his last duty assignment overseas, she'd told him she wanted to come home to a place where everyone knew her rather than live at some overseas military base and wait for him when he disappeared for weeks at a time.

He guessed he could understand it.

And being here the last couple of days, seeing how the town had pulled together after their stroke of good fortune, Sam could see what his wife saw in the place. He just wished he'd realized it a lot sooner.

Maybe then he wouldn't be standing on one bad leg and trying to figure out a way back into his wife's heart. And her bed.

But he hadn't counted on that long-haired hunk he'd seen with his hands all over his wife today. "Just Nick," she'd called him. *Just Nick?* Did Sam dare hope that it meant he wasn't someone special in Ruby's life? Did that mean Ruby *hadn't* moved on? Or did it mean she had so many guy friends that one, more or less, didn't matter?

Hell, Sam didn't know.

He parked his car on the road in front of Gwen's boardinghouse. No sense hiding it now. He'd kept the sports car stored at Tex's Garage while he was over-seas, and it had been hard as hell not to take her out and drive while he'd been keeping a low profile. Now that Ruby knew he was back, he guessed there wasn't much point in keeping it or himself out of sight.

Ruby knew where to find him now. It was up to her. He just hoped she'd call him soon. Otherwise he'd have to come up with a plan. And he didn't have a clue what that would be.

He slammed the car door shut, leaving the John Deere cap and the fleece-lined denim jacket he'd used as camouflage on the seat, and limped up the walk to the boardinghouse. Gwen Tanner, looking frazzled and pale, her auburn hair coming undone from its usual upswept do, was in the entranceway, and he greeted her.

"Hello, Gwen," he said simply. Gwen was about the same age as Ruby. However, her face had filled out, and she seemed to have grown plumper than he remembered.

"Sam? Sam Cade? What are you doing here?" Gwen walked over to him, and Sam could see why she appeared plumper. The woman was obviously pregnant. When had she gotten married?

"I'm in the spare room," he said, deciding to skirt the pregnancy issue for the time being. Since he'd wanted to get the "lay of the land" before going to see Ruby, he'd registered as S.C. Samuels and had paid for a week's stay in cash. It hadn't taken much to come into town under the radar. He hadn't recog-nized the woman who'd checked him in when he'd arrived a week ago, and she hadn't known him. He made a point of staying out of sight after that. When a special operations combat controller went covert and didn't want to be noticed, he wasn't. "I came for Ruby."

Now that Sam had made his presence known to Ruby, he figured it would be best to get his intentions out in the open. If that Nick guy was his competition, Sam intended for the man to know what he was up against. He just didn't want to force a confrontation. And the more people who knew he was here to get his wife back, the better.

Sam needed as many people on his side as he could get.

"Now? After all that time?"

"Better late than never," he said.

As he looked at the consternated expression on Gwen's face, he had to wonder.

RUBY STUMBLED OUT OF BED at the crack of dawn, worn out from a second night of restless sleep. It had been two days since Sam had shown up unannounced at her door, and she was still no closer to knowing how she felt about it. She was pretty sure she accepted his explanation. She'd lived with the man long enough to know that he wasn't a liar.

But what to do about it was another question. Her redheaded temper had caused her to fly off the handle and she'd filed for the divorce without really thinking the idea through. This time, by God, she was going to be sure before she did anything drastic.

It hadn't been easy filing for divorce, but as the days had passed, the hurt had lessened. She'd learned to live without Sam. After all, she'd had plenty of practice. She'd also learned that she didn't want to be alone.

When she'd seen him walking away the other day,

it had all but broken her heart. The hurt she'd felt at learning he'd broken his promise had come sneaking back, but all her love and desire for him had come flooding back, as well. And she wasn't sure which feeling was stronger.

Ruby splashed cold water on her face and ran a comb quickly through her hair. Still yawning and shivering in the morning chill, she made her way to the kitchen.

The smell of fresh coffee was enough to urge her on. Nick must have beaten her to the kitchen this morning and made the coffee. She'd have to thank him. As if all the help he'd given her in putting this place in order hadn't been enough!

At the kitchen door, she leaned wearily against the jamb, closed her eyes and breathed in the reviving aroma of freshly brewed coffee. Nick was definitely a lifesaver this morning.

"Good morning, Ruby."

"Sam?" She forced her sleepy eyes wide open. Sam was sitting at her kitchen table, looking as comfortable as if he belonged there. As he always had.

When he was at home.

"I let myself in," he said simply. "I didn't know when you'd be up, but I made the coffee. I know how you like it—rich and strong." He got up, went to the coffeepot and poured a cup. "Here. It looks like you need it," he said, holding it out to her.

Ruby wasn't sure whether to be grateful or insulted. Sam had as much as said that she looked like something the cat had dragged in—a far cry from the perfectly attired businesswoman she'd been when they'd met years ago. So she simply murmured, "Thank you," and accepted the mug.

Her chilly fingers closed around the warm porcelain and she breathed in the fragrant steam. "I'd forgotten how cold it can be in the mornings this late in spring," she muttered inanely, at a loss to understand her soon-to-be ex-husband's presence in her house this early in the day. "How did you get in?" she suddenly demanded.

"The door wasn't locked."

Of course. Nobody locked their doors way out here in rural Montana. Not unless there was a reason to. Was having a husband show up after months away a reason to lock the door, as she would if a convict were on the loose? With all the strangers in town these days, maybe she'd better start. She was alone here most of the time…Ruby realized. "It will be from now on."

Sam frowned. "I waited for you to call me, but you didn't. So I figured I'd come to you." He took a sip of his own coffee, then put the mug down. "I want you back, Ruby. We were good together."

"When we were together."

"I told you, I left the air force. I'm here to stay," Sam said, placing both hands palm down on the table in front of him. "That life is over."

"For how long?" Ruby looked down into her coffee and watched the rich liquid swirl. Whenever she looked at Sam, that old longing returned. She had to work this out with her brain, not her body. When she was close to Sam, her hormones clicked in and she couldn't think clearly.

"Forever."

"I wish I could believe that, Sam," Ruby said tiredly. "But what's to keep you from taking off as soon as something more exciting than raising organic vegetables comes up?" She took another sip of her coffee, hoping that the reviving brew would give her the strength she needed to face him.

"You gave me your word before," she added, "and we both know what happened. I need you to prove it to me. I can't take anything you say on faith anymore."

Sam looked as though she had struck him, and Ruby felt a pang of regret, but it had to be said.

"I want you to understand, Ruby, that I meant every word of that promise when I made it," he insisted, the expression on his face sobering. "But circumstances made it impossible to keep."

"I know that, Sam." Ruby stared at him, waiting, hoping for a real explanation. One that would magically make everything all right again. One that would erase the last painful five months.

"All right," he said slowly, making it clear that he was going to make no excuses. "I accept that I'm on probation, then. I mean it, Ruby. I'll do anything it takes to prove to you that my word is good and that I'm here to stay."

"Anything?"

Sam nodded. "Anything."

"Will you get up at the crack of dawn and shovel compost and manure? There's a lot of very dirty work involved in getting this farm producing." Ruby was testing him, and she fervently hoped he'd pass.

"I'm here. Have your way with me," he drawled, his smile wide and maddeningly cocksure.

Ruby rolled her eyes at the double entendre. It was so like the Sam she'd fallen in love with.

Was in love with still.

"Oops. Maybe I'd better come back later," a voice said.

Nick stood in the doorway from the mudroom to the kitchen. How much had he heard? "No, Nick, come in. Sam's going to be helping us get the farm working."

Nick stepped inside, taking off his Stetson. "Glad for the help, man," he said. He offered Sam his hand.

"Sam Cade," Sam said, accepting the handshake.

"Nick Folger." Each man eyed the other as though sizing him up. "Ruby's told me a lot about you."

"I wish I could say the same about you," Sam said wryly as he released Nick's hand.

As the two men took one another's measure, Ruby did the same. Sam and Nick were similar in height and build, with Nick being maybe an inch or two taller than Sam's six feet. Sam's muscular build had come from hard training, working out in a gym, while Nick's was from construction work. The biggest difference was, of course, their hair. Sam's dark brown hair was regulation trim, now salted with a bit of gray, and Nick's black mane was long and shiny and tied back with leather thong. And Nick had a silver-and-turquoise earring with a Native American motif in his left ear, something Sam would never dream of wearing.

"Nick's in construction in Rapid City," Ruby stated. "He's been indispensable in getting this place into shape." She turned toward the refrigerator. "I'll get breakfast ready, and then we can get started," she said as she got out a carton of eggs and a package of bacon.

"You don't have to cook breakfast for me, Ruby," Sam said. "I ate at Gwen's."

Ruby looked up as Nick poured himself a cup of coffee. She turned to Sam. "That reminds me… The apartment above the Mercantile is empty. There's no need for you to stay at the boardinghouse."

"Well, darlin'. I'd sort of planned on being able to stay here," Sam said, flashing one of his little boy grins that she had always been helpless to resist.

But not now! She'd gotten stronger in the months they'd been separated. "No, Sam," she told him firmly. "We are legally separated. Until—no, if—I decide otherwise, you will not stay under my roof."

Sam's grin faded a little, but he seemed undaunted. "Fair enough," he said. "I don't like it, but I can understand your logic. I'm paid up for the rest of the week at Gwen's, anyway. Then I just might take you up on that offer."

Ruby was pretty sure that Sam hoped for a different sort of invitation by the time he moved out of the boardinghouse, but until she was certain about his intentions, she was not about to let him come any closer to her than he was now. It was just too hard to be in the same room with him and not want him.

She would work beside him, she would cook his meals, but she wouldn't let him get close to her. She couldn't risk it. Not until she was sure about him.

Not until she was certain he would really stay this time.

Chapter Three

Sam laid the hammer down and flexed his tired arm. He guessed he was well on the way to working at the plan, if a man could consider working like a dog at a woman's beck and call a plan. But he had to prove to Ruby that he was willing to do things her way this time. They'd done it his way for the last ten years.

He glanced over at Nick, who was hammering away as if he had a bionic arm, then grabbed another board. Sam wasn't going to let that guy show him up. He was airborne. He could handle any situation put in front of him.

Even working on a farm.

Ruby had to learn that she could trust him. That when he made a promise, he meant it. That's why he was here, working his fingers to the bone and trying to keep up with—no, do more than—"Just Nick." Sam had to prove to Ruby that his word was his bond. Even if he had let her down in the past.

He'd never thought nailing a few boards would be such work, but if that six-foot gorilla, Nick, could do it, dammit, so could he. If Nick could knock together ten sets of cold frames—whatever they were—in a day, then Sam would do twelve. He just figured he'd better stop by Cozy's Drugstore on the way home and pick up some Epsom salts. He was definitely going to need to soak the aches out of the sore muscles he'd only just discovered he had.

He longed to take a break, but Nick was over on the other side of the yard hammering nails like an automaton. When was the man gonna let up? There was no way in hell Sam would quit before Nick did. Even if it killed him.

He'd be damned if he'd let that long-haired hippie get the best of him. But at this rate, he was pretty sure it was gonna kill him.

Sam hammered the last nail into the last board on this cold frame and stood back to examine his creation. It looked as if it would make a good sandbox. "What is a cold frame, anyway?" he mumbled as he gathered up his tools and supplies.

"It's a framework to let me plant early and to protect the young seedlings from the cold in early spring," Ruby said from somewhere behind him.

Sam turned to see her standing behind him, one hand on her hip, the other shading her eyes from the afternoon sun. She appeared to be evaluating his work.

"With a sandbox?"

Ruby laughed, a sound Sam used to love, but he wasn't sure, this time, if his wife was laughing at him or with him. "It's not finished yet. Nick's going to make tops covered with sheets of clear plastic that can be raised or lowered depending on the temperature."

Sam frowned. Was Nick going to make the tops today, after all the bottoms they'd already done? Sam would never get a break! "Oh," he said, feeling like a doofus and a half.

He was going to have to bone up on farming so he wouldn't keep looking like an imbecile in front of the woman he was trying to impress. At least he'd managed to make it through the day without collapsing in a heap on the ground.

Though he wished he could.

"Well, you've done a good day's work, Sam," Ruby said, sounding more like a picky employer than his loving wife. But Sam would take any encouraging word he could get from her. "Supper's almost done. Put your tools away and wash up, and we'll be ready to eat."

"Yes, ma'am," he said, with a snappy salute as she strolled away, leaving him a nice view of her well-shaped bottom in those worn, snug jeans. He felt more like a green recruit being ordered about by a drill sergeant than a valued member of Ruby's team, but he'd do as he was told. Ruby wanted to be in charge of him, and by God, he'd let her. Even if it killed him. As he headed for the toolshed, he tried to shake the stiffness out of his hammering arm, and thought it just might have.

Sam sure hated taking orders from Ruby, much less "Just Nick," and he wondered if all this groveling and hard work would pay off. He glanced back over his shoulder to where his priceless Ruby was hurrying into the house.

Yes, if she was gonna be the prize, it would definitely be worth it!

But at least he'd get to eat supper with the boss, he thought as he removed his tool belt and hung it on a hook in the shed. Hopefully, Nick would be eating elsewhere, but considering the way he'd showed up at breakfast and lunch, Sam wasn't sure he could count on that.

There was a utility sink in the shed, with a bar of soap perched on the rim. Sam pushed his sleeves up above his elbows and began to scrub. The water was cold, but he was hot, so it didn't matter that much in the scheme of things. If he were running this farm, though, he'd set up a hot water tank and a shower to use to keep from tracking mud and grime into the house.

Maybe he'd mention it to Ruby. If he could impress her with some useful ideas, it could go a long way toward changing her mind. He hoped.

Satisfied that he'd gotten most of the sweat and grime off, Sam splashed water on his face and head and dried off with paper towels hanging above the sink. Tomorrow he'd bring a clean shirt to put on after work. He sure wasn't going to impress his wife if he came in smelling like a farm worker every night. Even if that's what he was.

Cheered by his two good ideas, Sam hurried across the yard to the mudroom door.

He hadn't really taken the time to look at the kitchen, but he did now as he paused in the doorway. The appliances were all in that awful pea soup–green that had been popular when he was a kid. They might function, but they were ugly as all get out, and probably about ready to fall apart. Funny, though, the color seemed to suit Ruby, setting off her fiery-red hair with just the right contrast.

She was at the stove, stirring something. Maybe this was a good time to mention the shower thing. "Hey, I had a brainstorm out there in the shed," Sam said as he stepped inside. He hurried on. "How about installing a water heater in the toolshed? And maybe a shower, too."

"Already thought of that," Nick said, and Sam was not happy to notice that the man was already seated at the table. Hell, he'd even beaten him to his good idea. "Had to order the stuff out of Rapid City. Pine Run didn't have what I was looking for."

Damn, and Sam thought he'd been so smart. He stepped over to Ruby and held up his hands. "Do I pass inspection, boss?"

Ruby barely glanced up from the steaming pot of chili, which must have been cooking since they'd eaten lunch. "You're fine. Sit down. I'll put this on the table."

Sam sat.

Day one was over, and as far as he could tell, he was no closer to winning his wife than he'd been yesterday. But he'd do it.

If it was the last thing he did.

IT WAS SO HARD to act normal with Sam sitting there at her table as if nothing were wrong, but Ruby did what she could to keep from being moved by him. She'd always been turned on by the smell of her husband fresh from the shower, and with his short, dark hair slicked down with water, and droplets on his denim shirt, Sam looked as though he'd done his best to clean up for her. She was afraid if she got too close she'd get a whiff of soap from her freshly washed husband and it would all be over.

Maybe the four-alarm chili would overpower the scent of the man.

Ruby grabbed a couple of potholders from the

counter and carried the chili to the table, setting it on a trivet in the center. She'd serve her meals family style, and maybe she wouldn't have to get too close to Sam. At least, not until she was ready.

She returned to the stove, removed a skillet full of cornbread and turned it over a plate. She probably should have made a salad, she thought as she sliced the bread into wedges, but lettuce was hard to come by this time of year, and she wouldn't be up to full production of her own garden greens for some time. She had washed a dozen or so small carrots she'd pulled from her first crop, and they were already on the table.

"This is it, guys," she said as she carried the plate of cornbread to the table. "Eat up."

"Sure looks good," Nick said appreciatively.

"Yeah, it does. Ruby, you always did make the best chili and cornbread," Sam said in his best Georgia drawl. He turned to Nick. "Her chili is famous around the world. She's served it to combat controllers everywhere."

Ruby felt her face grow warm, though why a compliment from Sam would do that to her, she didn't know. "Thank you," she managed to say. "Chili isn't that hard."

"I've enjoyed Ruby's chili for years," Nick said, ladling some into a bowl.

Sam started to eat, but he stopped and glanced quizzically at Nick. Ruby wondered why, but Sam didn't explain his odd look, and she wasn't about to ask. She just wanted to get this meal over and done with and both men out of her kitchen and her house.

She needed peace and quiet to think.

Why had Sam decided to leave the service now? Why couldn't he have done it three years ago?

Ruby sighed and tried to eat. Suddenly, she didn't have much appetite, and she was pretty sure that Sam was the cause. And, she realized, she was a worse mess than she'd originally thought, if Sam had her off her feed.

"What made you decide to buy this farm?" Sam asked abruptly. "Wasn't the store enough to keep you busy?"

Ruby looked up from idly stirring her bowl of chili. "I needed a change," she said simply. She wasn't about to tell him that she needed to get away from the place that held so many memories of the two of them together, even if their time in the little apartment above the store had been limited.

"Kind of a big one, wouldn't you say? Taking on an old, beat-up house and going into farming," Sam observed.

"You know I've always loved to grow things. And this was the only place available." She shrugged. "So what if the house is a fixer-upper? I had the money, and Nick had the time."

And she'd needed a really big challenge to keep her from second-guessing her decision.

Of course, with Sam sitting across from her right now, she'd started worrying about it all over again.

"DINNER WAS GREAT, Ruby," Sam said after a second helping of the spicy chili.

Ruby blushed, looking pleased at the compliment, but said nothing more than a murmured, "Thanks." She seemed to be avoiding looking at him, and Sam wondered if that was a good sign or a bad one.

He thought just maybe it was a good sign. After all, he'd always been able to read Ruby's thoughts in those emerald-green eyes of hers, and she knew it. If Ruby was trying to keep him from looking into their verdant depths, then maybe it was because she was thinking something she didn't want him to know. And Sam didn't think it was that she wanted him to get lost. That notion cheered him immensely.

Nick echoed his sentiments about the chili, and Sam shot him a glare that was intended to say, "Stay off my turf," but Nick didn't even seem to notice.

"I don't suppose there's any dessert," Sam asked hopefully. Anything to give him a reason to stay longer. Anything to keep him as a barrier between Ruby and Nick. Though he'd seen nothing that indicated they wanted to be closer, he still wasn't taking any chances.

"Nope. Not today," Ruby said. "Didn't have time."

"Coffee?"

Ruby smiled as if she'd figured out what he was doing. "No. It'll keep me awake. I need all the beauty sleep I can get."

"No, you do not," Sam argued. "You'd be just as beautiful if you'd been up for a week," he said sincerely.

"Don't be ridiculous," Ruby said, blushing again. "I'm thirty-two years old. I need lots of beauty sleep. Besides, working on this farm is hard work."

"Amen to that one," Sam said.

Nick said nothing. He just chewed on a toothpick and watched, an enigmatic smile on his face.

Sam had hoped that Nick would have taken the hint and cleared out after dinner, but he showed no sign of budging. Since Ruby hadn't produced dessert and coffee, Sam figured he'd best be on his way. There was a fine line between being a squeaky wheel and a nuisance. The squeaky wheel might eventually get the oil, but a nuisance just might get tossed out.

He was hoping that Nick would soon fall into the nuisance category. Real soon.

He'd do well to remember that, Sam told himself as he headed reluctantly to the door. Absence made the heart grow fonder, and he sure hoped by clearing out early, Ruby would wonder…what? What could have happened?

Sam paused at the door. "Thanks for dinner, Ruby." He turned to Nick. "Good working with you."

Nick just nodded, and Sam felt he had to say something else to Ruby. "Same time in the morning, then?"

Ruby, who seemed distracted, looked up. "What?"

"Do you want me here at the same time tomorrow?" he repeated, more slowly this time.

"Oh, no. Nick's taking me to Pine Run to pick up some supplies. He has the truck," she said by way of explanation. "Since the Seed 'n Feed in Jester closed, we have to go to Pine Run for that sort of stuff. The hardware store doesn't have everything we need so it's easier to go to Pine Run than wait for Faulkner's to get it," Ruby explained. "I expect it will be an all-day trip."

"Anything you need me to do out here?"

"Not a thing that can't wait," Ruby said.

A day off was not what he wanted. He'd much rather be going to Pine Run with Ruby, but Sam knew this would be a battle he couldn't win. Couldn't get much in the way of supplies into his Corvette. And so far, Sam had seen no indication that Nick was making moves on his wife. He just hoped Nick wouldn't wait until they were out of town and out of sight.

Considering the stiffness in muscles he hadn't used in a long time, maybe he could use the time to recuperate and regenerate. And he'd go to the library, or maybe Ex-Libris, the bookstore, and see what he could learn about farming. He feigned a salute, turned and headed out into the falling darkness.

Damn, he wished there was a way to get rid of that Nick fellow. Or at least know what his intentions were. It was too damned soon to confront the man. But Sam sure would like to know what Nick was up to, especially since he and Ruby were going to be alone together all day tomorrow. Ruby had won a lot of money. What if Nick was just itching to get his hands on it?

A million dollars might seem like a pretty good motive for a man to woo a woman, even one half as beautiful as Ruby. Sam would have to keep an eye on "Just Nick."

Sam slid into the Corvette and started the engine. He had to come up with a way to show Ruby that he meant what he'd told her about staying, he decided. A sure sign of his intention to stay would be to get rid of the Corvette and replace it with a more practical vehicle. The Corvette might be great on the open highway, especially with Montana's "reasonable speed" laws, but it sure wasn't fit for these back country roads.

But he loved this car, he thought as he drove slowly out onto the rutted dirt road that led from the house to the highway. He wouldn't do anything rash right now.

As he drove slowly through town, he noticed signs of the new prosperity brought by the lottery win. Some of the street names had changed, but it was more than just renaming streets Mega-Bucks Boulevard or Lottery Lane. The shabbiness seemed to have gone—as had the old pavilion in the park. It had looked as though it was ready to fall down last time he'd visited Ruby in Jester. Maybe it had collapsed before the town had come into its unexpected good fortune.

It seemed as if the townspeople and merchants had gone whole-hog and pulled out their Sunday best, dressing up the town to the nines. Hell, that corroded green horse statue in front of the town hall had been cleaned and polished until it shone like a new penny.

Sam laughed out loud. But, Cozy's Drugstore was already closed. He still couldn't get a box of Epsom salts on the way back to Gwen's. So much had changed, yet so little.

Still, if he was going to win his wife back, he was going to have to come to terms with the town of Jester, Montana—with what it had to offer and what it didn't. Ruby, for better or worse, loved it here, and he loved Ruby. He truly did. So he'd best get used to it.

Sam parked in front of the boardinghouse and went inside. He reckoned he'd have plenty of time to figure out just what he could do to make sure that Nick was out of the picture.

And he was back in it.

Chapter Four

"All right, Nick, you win, but four o'clock seems awfully early to eat." After her trip to Pine Run, Ruby let Nick talk her into stopping at the Brimming Cup for supper.

Her shopping expedition had been successful, but tiring, so she was just as happy to let Dan Bertram cook for her as to do it herself. But being in town made it more likely that she'd run into Sam. And she was still dealing with her feelings about Sam's sudden appearance in Jester after so long.

"It won't be that crowded yet, and besides, you're a woman of means," Nick said as he steered the truck into a parking slot in front of the diner. "You can afford to let others do for you now and then."

Ruby had almost talked herself into being excited about eating dinner in town, then she noticed who was coming out of Ex-Libris, the bookstore, just down the street. Sam!

Her husband had never been much of a reader, and Ruby couldn't imagine what he'd be doing at a bookstore. Of course, Amanda Devlin, the owner, kept a tray of goodies baked by Gwen Tanner on hand for her customers. And considering Sam's insatiable sweet tooth, maybe that was the reason. But he was carrying a paper sack. Amanda didn't sell cookies, just books. "I wonder what he's doing there," Ruby said, not realizing she'd voiced her curiosity out loud.

"Who?" Nick said, cutting the engine. He followed the direction of Ruby's gaze. "Oh. Sam."

Sam must have seen the truck, for he crossed the street and headed their way, raising a hand to wave. "So much for avoiding Sam all day," Ruby muttered as she pushed the truck door open. Besides, she wanted to know what her almost-ex-husband had clutched in the sack in his other hand.

He caught up with them in front of the Brimming Cup.

Hoping that Sam was just being friendly before continuing on his way to Gwen's boardinghouse, Ruby managed a smile. "I see you've been to the bookstore," she said, nodding in the direction of the bag.

"Yeah, thought I'd better bone up on organic farming," he said. "Got a couple of general interest books on gardening, and I ordered some on organics. I might have grown up in a farming community in Georgia, but my folks were schoolteachers," he continued by way of explanation. "And peanuts are not exactly the same as organic vegetables," he added.

"I see," Ruby said. She guessed she'd have to give Sam points for trying. "Does that mean you'll finally be able to tell the difference between a petunia and a pansy?" she added with a mischievous grin.

"Probably not, but I might be able to tell a daisy from a dandelion."

Ruby chuckled, and Nick arched an eyebrow in question, so she guessed she'd have to explain.

"Once when we were in base housing in Florida, Sam helped me weed a flower bed. However, he pulled all the plant seedlings and left the weeds."

"Well, the weeds were bigger...." Sam said, shrugging sheepishly.

"But the seedlings were all lined up in a row."

Nick looked as though he were trying to suppress a smile, but to his credit, he didn't laugh.

"Needless to say, I was not amused."

"Not amused? Hell, she threw a genuine hissy fit. And that's the last time Ruby asked me to help her with her flower beds."

"And I'm pretty sure you did that on purpose so I wouldn't ask you anymore," Ruby said, hitting Sam playfully on the arm. Then, realizing what she'd done, she shoved her hand self-consciously into her pocket.

Nick started to go into the diner, but Ruby shook her head slightly in a gesture she hoped Sam wouldn't notice. Dinner with Sam last night had been too strained, and she didn't want to do it again quite so soon. Gwen put on a good spread at the boarding-house. Ruby hoped that Sam would continue on to Gwen's and leave her and Nick to eat in peace.

"You going to eat at the Brimming Cup?" Leave it to Sam to get right to the point.

Ruby had no choice but to nod.

"Yeah," Nick said. "You want to join us?"

Ruby could have kicked him for issuing the invitation. Instead she shot him a pointed glare.

"Thank you. I think I will. Gwen is cooking up some French dish for supper. I wasn't looking forward to it." Sam all but shuddered, and Ruby smiled, remembering Sam's aversion to European cuisine. "I'm thinking a big fat burger sounds good."

"You would," Ruby muttered. Her husband had always been a meat-and-potatoes man. "Dan does cook up a good meat loaf. But it goes fast. We'd better get inside before the place fills up," she said, resigned. "I guess it is good that we're here so early. It can be standing room only on Friday nights." And the sooner they ate, the sooner she could make her excuses and head for home.

Of course, she'd still have to deal with her feelings about Sam—not to mention her sexual attraction to him—tomorrow when he showed up at the farm to work.

Nick pushed open the diner door and the bell tinkled, announcing their arrival. Ruby guessed there was no turning back now. There was no way she was going to offend Dan Bertram, the cook, by leaving. Though everyone in Jester knew that Dan's bark was far worse than his bite, he could come across like a pit bull and would surely grouse about her rudeness for weeks.

She'd do anything to prevent that. Even choke down a meal with her ex-husband.

The threesome stepped inside.

There were three spots open at the counter—not all side by side, Ruby noted—and none of the four tables or six booths were empty. She made a beeline for an empty stool beside Seth Hollis, who seemed more interested in waitress Valerie Simms than in his dinner. The stool on the other side was taken by a man she didn't know. Then someone touched her arm.

Ruby looked over her shoulder as Sam's hand closed around her elbow. "This one is about to be empty," he said, nodding toward a front booth at the large glass window, where a man was signaling to the waitress for his check.

Valerie hurried to the table with the bill. "I'll have this table cleaned up in a jiffy and you can sit," she said, glancing over her shoulder toward Sam.

"No hurry," he said pleasantly. Nick just watched as Valerie accepted the cash, made change and stepped back so the couple could leave.

As promised, Valerie had the table cleared and wiped down in no time. Sam gestured for Ruby to sit, and then slid in right beside her, giving Nick no choice but to take the bench across from them.

Maybe it was dirty pool, Sam thought, but he had to figure out a way to get close to Ruby. And near her he was. Though there was ample room on the padded, blue vinyl seat, he crowded close to her so that they were hip to hip. He felt a pleasant, electric tingle as he edged up to her and their bodies touched. Then he drew in a deep breath of the raspberry shower soap Ruby always used, and his groin tightened. He hadn't noticed it before. Had she saved it for the occasion of going to town? Or for Nick? Ruby seemed to stiffen, but she didn't draw away.

It was a damned good thing he was sitting down, or his feelings for his wife would be out there for all the good folks of Jester to see. Reluctantly, Sam scooted an inch or two away. He was still close enough so that a deep breath on either of their parts could leave them touching, but for now, he was safe.

He accepted the plastic-covered menu Valerie handed him, but only pretended to peruse it. He knew what he wanted: a fat, juicy burger and fries. And Ruby. And not necessarily in that order.

Ruby, too, seemed to be studying the menu. Sam

knew it was a pretense for his benefit, because the menu at the Brimming Cup probably hadn't changed in twenty years. If not longer. Ruby gnawed at her lip, a slight frown wrinkling her alabaster forehead, a sure sign that something was bothering her. Sam was pretty certain it wasn't what to pick from the restaurant menu.

He smiled to himself, then looked up at Valerie, who waited patiently, her order pad in hand. "I'll have a burger, rare, and fries," he said. "I don't suppose you could scare up some iced tea for me, could you, sugar?" He flashed her a grin.

Valerie looked puzzled. "Iced tea? That isn't on the menu."

Ruby smiled and shook her head slowly. "It's okay, Valerie. My darling husband is a foreigner. Where he comes from they have iced tea with everything."

"Not to mention co-cola for breakfast," Sam interjected, grinning. He loved the fact that she'd referred to him as her "darling husband." It just about made his day.

Making a face at Sam, Ruby continued. "Just bring Sam a cup of hot tea and a couple of glasses of ice. He can take it from there."

"Sure," Valerie said, then jotted down the other orders.

At least Ruby remembered what to do when good, sweet Southern iced tea wasn't available, Sam thought. If he was going to survive in this one-horse town, he was going to have to teach Dan how to make decent iced tea and cornbread. But, he guessed, he'd have to wait until he was certain he would be staying.

RUBY FELT AS THOUGH she'd been tied up in knots for hours instead of maybe thirty minutes. She poked at the pile of green beans left on her plate. Sitting so close to Sam had resurrected all those old feelings she'd hoped to suppress. Whenever she was close to him, her heart seemed to beat faster, the air seemed thinner and it was all she could do to eat. If she kept this up, she'd be nothing but skin and bones in the space of a week.

She looked away from the half-eaten meat loaf dinner, now cold and unappetizing, and sighed. She'd managed to swallow enough to keep from offending Dan, but what she'd eaten had tasted more like plastic packing peanuts than real food. The lack of flavor had nothing to do with Dan's good cooking or her desire for food, but the feelings for Sam that she still found impossible to quell.

It would be so easy to fall in love with him again— as if she had ever fallen out. It would be so easy to let Sam back into her life. But she would be holding her breath wondering if, one day, he'd decide that sleepy Jester, Montana, was too slow for him and he needed more excitement.

What was she going to do?

"You haven't eaten much, kid," Nick said. "What's got you off your feed?"

Ruby shook her head. "Nothing," she murmured. "Just tired after a busy day." Oh great, she thought. Just what she needed—having Nick point out that she hadn't eaten with her usual gusto. She knew full well that Sam would remember her lack of appetite meant she had something on her mind. "You know I had a big lunch in Pine Run," she added, hoping that Sam wouldn't see through her flimsy excuse. He knew she'd always had a healthy appetite.

And she knew that his confident military ego would allow him to see very quickly that he was the cause of her lack of appetite. He would be quick to take two and two and come up with four. He would have to know that she still wanted him.

She laid her fork down and sighed.

Sam covered her hand with his. "It's all right, Ruby. You don't have to eat if you don't want to."

Ruby wanted to pull her hand away. She hated the way Sam's touch made her skin tingle and turned her brain to mush. No, that was a lie. She loved it. She craved it, but she didn't want to feel that way now, when she needed to be able to think clearly. And she didn't need to show him that he bothered her so.

He already knew, anyway.

Sam patted her hand and signaled to Valerie. "How 'bout you fix up a piece of Shelly's Dutch apple pie over there to go? Ruby can have some later if she gets hungry."

Valerie looked at her for confirmation, and all Ruby could do was nod her head. There, he'd done it again. Sam knew that she was a sucker for Shelly Dupree O'Rourke's signature pie, and he knew that she'd be starved later. Valerie scurried away.

Sam patted her hand, and Ruby felt herself go all soft inside. The only thing that was keeping her from throwing herself in Sam's arms was the fact that they were sitting across the table from Nick. The only thing that was keeping her from begging Sam to take her and make mad, passionate love to her was that they were in full view of the staff and patrons of the Brimming Cup diner. And her own stubborn pride.

"Don't do that," she snapped, angry that Sam could evoke such sensations in the middle of a public diner.

"Sorry…!" Sam said. "You used to like it when I touched you."

He lifted his hand, and suddenly Ruby could think rationally again. At the same time, she felt oddly bereft at the loss of his touch. What was the matter with her? Why couldn't she look at the man who had so disappointed her, had driven her to the brink of divorce, without aching to be in his arms?

"I liked to eat library paste in second grade, but I got over it," Ruby retorted.

Valerie returned with a good-size piece of dessert on a cardboard plate, covered with plastic wrap. She handed it to Ruby. "Will there be anything else?"

"I reckon that'll do it," Sam said, taking charge as usual. He slid out of the booth and looked over at Nick. "You take our Ruby home and see to it that she gets plenty of rest, and I'll be out at the farm at first light."

Nick reached for his wallet, but Sam shook his head. "No, this one's on me," he said, and Ruby looked up with a start.

Ruby could feel Sam's eyes burning into hers. "Sam, I can certainly pay for my dinner," she protested.

"I know you can, Ruby," he said in that seductive Southern drawl of his. "But I reckon you'll need every penny of those lottery winnings to make that farm a go. Consider this my contribution to the cause."

"My winnings?" Ruby stared at him. He was looking so doggoned self-righteous. Why was he making such a big deal about the money?

"I have a big ol' military pension of my own. I can't live high on the hog, but I won't starve," Sam said, as if reading her mind, and Ruby wondered if he was making a point or merely making a comment.

Finally, Sam cleared his throat and spoke again. "So I reckon I can afford to spot you for dinner," he said, his voice unnaturally thick. "You go on home. I'm gonna have a piece of pie and a cup of coffee before I go," he told her. "I'll see you in the morning." Sam offered his hand, and Ruby accepted it as she slid out of the booth.

His touch made her tingle, but Ruby still had a long way to go before she'd trust him with her heart again. "Thank you for the pie," she murmured, the take-out pie clutched tightly in her hand.

Nick touched Ruby's waist and urged her toward the door. She glanced over her shoulder in time to see Sam sit back down in the booth, an expression she wasn't sure she could read on his face.

As Nick led her to the truck, all she could think about was Sam. Why had he sent her so cheerfully home, and why wasn't he trying to talk himself into her house…and her bed?

SAM WATCHED as Nick helped Ruby into the truck, then walked around and climbed in. Without so much as turning back to wave, Ruby fastened her seat belt, and Nick started the engine. Then they rode off with a truckful of the day's purchases. And what was left of Sam's heart. Damn, he hated the thought of having to go back to Gwen's boardinghouse and sleep alone when Ruby was within hollering distance.

"Sam Cade?"

He looked up, startled to find himself addressed by
name, to see a man in a sheriff's uniform standing by
the booth. He knew Ruby was upset that he'd reappeared in her life without any warning, but he hadn't
expected that she'd sic the sheriff on him.

Chapter Five

"I'm Sam Cade," he replied warily.

The man stuck out his hand. "Luke McNeil. Got a minute?"

They shook, each taking the measure of the other. "Sure. Have a seat. It's your town," Sam said, gesturing. It apparently wasn't official business if the sheriff was offering his hand, but Sam wouldn't put it past someone in town to have pointed out that he'd been skulking around, and have asked the sheriff to check him out.

"No, I just try to keep the peace in it," McNeil corrected as he slid into the booth across from Sam.

Valerie set a cup of coffee in a take-out container in front of the sheriff without being asked, and Luke waited until she had moved away before continuing. "Thought I could use your talents," he said.

Okay, it was official, but he wasn't the object of scrutiny. Sam fished in his pocket for money to pay the tab as McNeil took a sip of coffee. "How?"

Luke glanced around the busy diner, where the patrons seemed to be pretending to mind their own business. "Walk outside with me, Sam," he suggested, dropping a dollar bill on the table. Sam knew how

people in small towns always wanted to know everyone else's affairs. Whatever McNeil had to say, Sam
figured it wasn't for public consumption.

Sam collected his sack of books, and they stepped
outside to the tune of the bell jangling above the door.

"Where you staying?" Luke said, after putting on
his hat and glancing around.

The street had become as congested as it was pos-
sible to be in a small town like Jester, and obviously,
McNeil didn't want to be overheard. "Gwen's place.
What's up?"

Luke nodded in the direction of the boardinghouse.
"I'll walk with you and fill you in as we go."

His curiosity up and running, Sam waited in silence
as he and Sheriff McNeil strolled toward Gwen's.
Once they'd left the bustle of Main Street, Luke explained what he wanted. "You noticed that the pavilion in the park has collapsed."

Sam nodded.

"It wasn't an accident," Luke said.

"You sure? Considering the state of disrepair it
was in the last time I was in town, I figured it could
have fallen on its own."

"Some bolts were tampered with. Engineer's report
confirms it. And since somebody tried to burn it down
after that, there isn't much doubt in my mind."

Sam arched an eyebrow. Maybe there was more
excitement in little Jester than he'd thought. "Got any
idea who?"

"I have some suspects, but nothing concrete. Don't
have any real evidence that points to anyone. That's
where you come in. I noticed how you came into
town under the radar last week. Most other people
didn't, but they're not trained observers. I need you

to do a little nosing around for me. Since not everybody in Jester knows you, maybe you can pick up some undercurrent I've missed. Some clue.''

Sam shrugged. "I reckon I could help out. But Ruby and I have become the chief topic of conversation around here. You saw how everyone turned to look when we left the diner.''

"Yeah, but we weren't trying not to be noticed.'' Luke clasped Sam's shoulder. "Do what you can. I need an extra set of eyes and ears. And I get the feeling you won't be taking sides like some of the other people around here.''

"I'll give it my best,'' Sam said. "I just can't make any promises.''

"That's all I ask,'' Luke said, adjusting his hat. Then he turned and strode away, leaving Sam to wonder just what was happening in the sleepy Montana hamlet.

RUBY STUMBLED OUT of her bedroom and into the kitchen. This morning she was not greeted by the welcoming aroma of fresh-brewed coffee as she had been two days before. And today she really needed it.

She was going to have to get herself together about this Sam situation or she'd be among the walking wounded for the duration. She couldn't go on operating on too little sleep with too much on her mind.

Why had Sam come back now?

Why hadn't he been there for her six months ago, when it really mattered? Heck, for the past couple of years?

She went through the motions of making coffee, actions more on automatic pilot than with conscious effort. She loved her old-fashioned, blue-and-white-speckled enamel coffeepot, and she resisted the idea of getting one of those new ones that had a timer. Except on mornings like this.

Ruby took a seat at the kitchen table, propping her elbows on top and her tired head on her hands as she waited for the coffee to perk.

The smell of scorched coffee and the sizzle of liquid hitting the hot stove jerked her awake. Darn, she had fallen asleep, and the pot was boiling over. She turned off the gas, grabbed for a potholder and removed the coffee from the stove. "That's it. I've had it. I don't care if I miss an entire day of work on this farm, I am going to get an automatic coffeemaker. Today," she muttered as she swabbed at the mess on top of the stove.

"You mean one like this?" Sam asked as he walked in through the mudroom door.

"Wh—?"

"Good morning, Ruby," he said cheerfully, as he removed a brand-new, automatic coffeemaker from its box and proceeded to set it up on the counter.

"But—?"

"Consider it a housewarming gift from me," Sam said, his expression so doggoned cocky as he rinsed out the pot, then filled it with water. "You always hated to wait for the coffee to be ready in the morning." He found the ground coffee in the refrigerator, spooned it in, then pushed the hopper into position. "Hot coffee coming up," he said. "But then, we might have to experiment until we figure out how much to use to get it strong the way you like it."

All Ruby could do was watch. This was so like Sam, taking over as he was. And he'd always been able to read her mind. To know exactly what she was thinking. Even when she didn't want him to.

Why, then, had he been so stupid as to go on that mission, when he knew how much she hated it? Ruby finally found her voice. "Where did you get that?" she managed to croak.

"I picked it up at the Mercantile. I had thought I'd use it in the apartment, but then I figured you could use it more than me, sugar," Sam said in that honey-sweet Southern drawl of his. Just hearing it made Ruby go mushy all over. She had always loved the way he called her sugar. Now she wished he wouldn't. She needed to think about Sam with a clear head, not a brain made out of oatmeal.

"You did pay for it, didn't you?" was all Ruby could think to say in her befuddled state.

"Of course I did. You may have a low opinion of me, but I am an officer and a gentlemen. Or I was." His cockiness faded a little, and Ruby knew that his medical retirement was still a sore point.

And that worried her. So much of his ego had been tied up in his position as an officer in an elite team of special operations combat controllers. Would he get bored here and leave when something more exciting came up?

"You could say thank you, darlin'," Sam reminded her gently.

"Thank you, Sam. You always seem to know how to please me." Especially in bed, Ruby couldn't help thinking. She shook her head to get the notion out of it, and was glad when Nick came in. Thankfully, his being there made it possible for her to pull herself together. At least, Nick's presence seemed to dilute some of Sam's potent charms. "Okay, I'm making breakfast," she said. "Who's hungry?"

Nick raised his hand, but Sam simply crossed his arms over his chest and leaned against the counter near the coffee machine, his legs crossed at the ankles, a smug look on his face.

"I already ate," he finally said. "But I'm still hungry," he added so softly that Ruby was probably the only one who heard.

And she also knew that she was the only one who'd been meant to hear. Sam wasn't hungry for eggs and bacon.

He wanted her.

Ruby drew in a deep breath and set about making breakfast for Nick and herself, even though she knew she wouldn't eat it. She was hungry, too. And, dog-gone it, not for breakfast. She still wanted Sam as much as she ever had, and that could be her ruination.

Or maybe her salvation.

Why did this all have to be so darned confusing?

SAM LOOKED UP from where he'd been turning over the recently started compost heap and watched as Ruby laughed and joked with Nick. The bright morning sun made her copper-colored hair gleam like a new penny as she threw her arms around Nick in an exuberant hug, and it was all Sam could do to keep his eyes off her.

Damn that Nick, Sam thought as he stabbed a pitchfork into the compost as hard as he could.

That green-eyed monster Sam had been trying to keep in the back of his mind jumped out, front and center. Ruby had been taking pains to avoid him, and when she was around him, she acted all stiff and formal, as if they hadn't spent ten good years together. Yet with Nick, she laughed and carried on as if they'd known each other forever. Sam leaned on the pitch-fork and squinted to see if he could read their lips and tell what they were talking about.

He'd been able to piece together, as best he could without asking directly, that though Nick was taking his meals with Ruby, he was sleeping in that beat-up travel trailer. But Sam wondered how long that would have lasted if he hadn't turned up when he had. Was Nick angling for the place in Ruby's bed that Sam had always occupied?

No, he couldn't think that. He and Ruby were not divorced yet, and he knew his wife well enough that he was certain she would not invite another man into her bed until she was legally free to do so. And it was up to Sam to make sure that didn't happen.

The subjects of his surveillance must have sensed he was watching them, because they both turned and waved. Sam waved back. What else could he do?

He picked up the pitchfork and attacked the pile of half-rotted hay with a vengeance, wishing heartily that it was Nick he was battling. How was he going to convince Ruby to give him another chance, with Nick hanging around all the time? He hadn't had a private moment with Ruby yet. Sam stabbed at the pile of hay and flung the stuff farther than necessary. Here he was, a highly trained commando, well versed in all kinds of computer and electronic technology, and he was shoveling hay, while Nick was getting all the good jobs and romancing his wife.

As he worked, Sam felt the short hairs on the back of his neck begin to rise, a sure sign that he need-ed to be alert. He looked up to see that Ruby was heading his way. Their eyes met and held, then she looked away.

Sam wondered why. Was it because she was guilty about carrying on with Nick, or was it because the old attraction between them was still pulling them together, as strongly as ever? He stabbed the fork into the pile of hay and leaned on it, waiting for Ruby to approach, and appreciating the way the worn denim hugged her hips and did nothing to disguise her slender shape. She might be dressed like a man to work this farm, but she was all woman.

And she was his. At least, she would be again, or he would die trying.

Ruby smiled as she drew near, shading her eyes with her hands in the strong noontime sun. "You can stop now," she said. "I think it's dead."

Sam laughed, appreciating the fact that she'd finally loosened up a little with him. "Yeah, you can't be having a killer compost heap lurking around your farm. No tellin' what would happen."

"No telling," Ruby said, propping her elbows on a fence that showed evidence of recent repair. She stared off into the distance as she leaned against it.

"I thought I heard around town that you were going to raise hogs," Sam commented, when Ruby didn't explain why she'd come over.

"I thought so, too," she replied, still wearing that faraway look. "Then I met Petunia and the kids."

"Petunia and the kids? Do you have some other farm workers here I don't know about?"

Ruby chuckled and turned back to face him. "No, Petunia is a pig. Hog, I guess. She and an old boar were the only stock left on this spread when I bought it. I had thought to buy more, hog prices being what they are, but then I met Petunia.'' She sighed, and Sam appreciated the way her chest rose and fell, straining against her chambray work shirt. ''She'd just had a litter of piglets, and they were so cute....'' Her voice trailed off.

''You couldn't bear the thought of sending them to slaughter,'' Sam concluded.

Ruby shuddered and glanced back to where she'd been looking before. ''Don't say that word. It gives me the willies! Yes, Petunia is so sweet, and the piglets are so cute. All I could think about was Arnold the pig on that television show *Green Acres,* and maybe Piglet from *Winnie the Pooh.*'' She sighed again. ''I just couldn't bear the thought of it.''

She turned back to face him and grinned. ''So I dropped the idea of raising pigs and went back to the original plan—organic vegetables.''

''And spared Petunia's life.'' Sam looked around. He had seen no evidence of pigs since he'd been there. ''Did you give them away? Petunia and the kids, I mean.'' And the boar, too, he supposed.

Ruby's grin faded. ''Roscoe died. We found him out in the woods right after I took possession of the farm. Gave him a decent burial. Melinda Hartman, the vet, said that Roscoe had run wild for years and was probably quite old. Nobody had been able to catch him.''

''Except Petunia,'' Sam said.

''Yes. And that was probably his last hurrah,'' Ruby said wryly.

''Yeah, but what a way to go.'' Sam grinned. He couldn't help making that comment. He'd always assumed he'd die at home in bed, with Ruby beside him, when he was eighty or ninety or maybe even a hundred. His own brush with mortality had made him think about that a lot lately, not take it for granted as he had in the past.

"Anyway, Petunia and the kids pretty much have the run of the place for now. They're out there somewhere," Ruby said, pointing in the direction she'd been looking. "We figured getting them fenced in properly could wait a little longer while we got the place ready for the first crop. They'd survived this long without us and could probably hang on a little longer."

But Sam wasn't sure he would. Talking about Petunia's and the late Roscoe's amorous adventures had done nothing to quench the ardor he still felt for his wife.

Ruby turned to him. "I wanted to tell you how much I've appreciated your help, Sam," she said, reverting to that stiff formality he'd hoped had finally gone. "With you taking care of the small stuff, Nick's been able to get a lot more done."

Sam tipped the cap that protected him from the strong Montana sun. "Anytime, ma'am," he said. "I aim to please." He'd much rather please Ruby another way, but he'd have to bide his time for that.

At least he'd gotten through to her during those few unguarded moments. Maybe she'd begin letting her defenses down soon.

Ruby laughed, and Sam loved hearing it. "I'm going to go put lunch together. I think that compost heap has been turned enough. Get washed up, then come in and eat."

"Yes, ma'am." Sam saluted, hefted the pitchfork into position on his shoulder and marched toward the toolshed. Yep, he thought as he watched Ruby stroll toward the house. Maybe he was beginning to see a tiny chink in her protective armor. All he had to do now was figure out how to make it big enough to let him in.

If he could only get rid of Nick, that task would be a hell of a lot easier. Since Sam wasn't about to resort to murder, he'd have to find some other way to get the man out of the picture.

And a faster way to get back into Ruby's good graces.

SHE'D ALWAYS KNOWN that Sam was a hard worker, but Ruby wondered what had him so fired up that he'd been attacking that pile of half-rotted hay as if his life depended on it. She tried to figure out what was going on in her husband's head as she assembled sandwiches and laid them out on a platter for lunch.

"He's a hard worker," Nick said. "You have to give him that."

"Yeah," Ruby said, trying to shove a lock of hair out of her eyes with her shoulder. Her hands were full and she couldn't get it herself.

Nick must have noticed, for he stepped closer and brushed the errant strand away from her face, tucking it securely behind her ear. "There," he said. "All better."

They turned quickly at the sound of a quick gasp of breath.

Sam had come in. He glared at Nick, and Ruby wondered what that was all about, but he didn't explain and she didn't ask. Instead, she took a closer look at him.

His hair was wet and slick from washing, and damp spots dotted his shirt. A clean one, Ruby noticed with surprise. Especially for her? He'd changed into a clean T-shirt and, just like the other day, he smelled like soap. Just thinking about Sam fresh from the shower made her feel all warm and mushy.

Ruby shook that thought from her head as she turned back to finish making the lemonade. She had to stop thinking about that. She and Sam had a lot to work through before she'd be able to accept him back into her life for good.

Nick stepped quickly away from her, and Sam silently took his place. He stood so close behind her that Ruby could feel his warm breath on her neck. She should have been annoyed at his blatant act of possession, but instead she felt shivers of delight skittering down her spine.

Ruby felt Sam's hands on her waist and then he began to skim them up her side just as he used to do when things were happier, when their marriage was...what? Real? In the old days he would have ended this sensory exploration with a kiss at the curve of her neck, and Ruby almost leaned in to receive it.

"Lunch ready?" Nick asked, interrupting the moment.

They sprang apart guiltily, though what they had to be guilty for, Ruby didn't know. Technically, she and Sam were still married.

"That lemonade will sure hit the spot today," Nick said as he took a seat at the table.

"Yeah," Sam agreed. "I wouldn't have expected things to get so hot when it's been so cold the last few days." Something told Ruby that he wasn't talking about the weather.

"It's always like that this time of year," Ruby said, as if she hadn't understood Sam's insinuation. Why couldn't they just speak about what really mattered instead of making stupid chitchat about the weather?

She knew why. What had to be said between her and Sam was best done without a third party listening. She loved Nick, but he was proving to be something of a fifth wheel here. She and Sam really needed some time alone in neutral territory. Although she just wasn't sure she would be able to handle it.

Ruby drew a deep breath, picked up the pitcher of freshly made lemonade and carried it to the table. ''Anybody thirsty?'' she asked brightly.

Two dark heads nodded, and Ruby passed the pitcher to Sam, who seemed to make certain their hands touched. As the familiar heat sizzled through her, Ruby let go. No, she couldn't trust herself to be alone with Sam. Not until she was sure he was here to stay.

And how the heck she was going to be able to do that when she couldn't be in the same room with him without thinking about hot summer nights and rumpled sheets, she didn't know.

AFTER SUPPER THAT NIGHT, Sam pushed back his chair and sighed with satisfaction. Again he'd put in a long day of work on Ruby's farm, and again Nick wouldn't give him the pleasure of a moment alone with his wife. Sam was beginning to sense that Ruby might actually be sharing those same sentiments. It wasn't the entire campaign, but any little victory won, even one as seemingly insignificant as this one, was one step closer to winning the war. ''Dinner was great, as usual, Ruby,'' he said as he clambered to his feet.

There didn't seem to be any dessert forthcoming,

so he might as well get along. And when would Ruby have had time to make dessert, anyway? It still surprised him that she was able to manage what meals she did. She put in almost as much time and hard work out there as he and Nick.

Sam figured he was ready to initiate part two of the plan. It was the absence-makes-the-heart-grow-fonder play. From the dinner conversation, he could tell that Ruby and Nick were expecting him to be here tomorrow, even though it would be Sunday.

He would not be here.

Sam was still waiting for the perfect opening to drop his little bombshell, but if it didn't present itself soon, he'd just go ahead and drop it anyway.

The old black wall phone behind Ruby rang, and she jerked, clearly startled. Then she reached back to answer it. "It's for you, Nick," she said after a moment.

"I'll take it in the office," he said. He strode away toward the interior of the house.

Sam pushed back an irritating twinge of jealousy. He hadn't even known there was an office in the house. What was Nick doing in the nether reaches of Ruby's house, when he, Sam, had not been beyond the kitchen or the living room?

But at least it gave him a brief moment alone with his wife.

Ruby, listening with her hand over the mouthpiece, got out of her chair to hang up, leaving them both standing with nothing to say and nowhere to go. She turned to Sam, wiped her hands on the front of her faded jeans and presented him with a hopeful smile. "Will I see you first thing in the morning, then?"

Sam couldn't help smiling inwardly. Now was the

perfect moment to play hard-to-get as part of his plan. "Nope," he said firmly. "I have other plans."

He hoped his announcement might make her jealous, but if she asked what his plans were he would tell her.

Her eyes widened in surprise, if only briefly, and then she seemed to compose herself. "Will I see you on Monday, then?" Did Ruby sound disappointed? Sam wondered.

He thought so. And he decided to let her off the hook. "I'm paid up at Gwen's through tonight. Tomorrow I'll move into the apartment above the Mercantile," he said simply. "I'll need the time to move my belongings in and get organized."

"Oh, I see." Ruby hooked her fingers in her belt loops as if she were trying to look casual. She seemed relieved, if Sam was any judge—and he'd had so much practice he could read his wife like a book. "There isn't much in the way of dishes and cookware, but there's a bed and chairs to sit on. If you need anything else, ask me. After all, half of this is really yours." She jerked her head in the direction of the interior of the house.

"I don't need much," Sam said. "Just a place to sleep and hang my hat. I'm sure I'll be fine." He stepped into the mudroom, took his cap off the hook and jammed it on his head. "See ya," he said. Then he left her standing alone in the kitchen.

Sam sensed that he had really gotten to Ruby. For what it was worth, his wife had seemed disappointed that he wouldn't be at the farm tomorrow, and that pleased him no end.

Of course, that left her there alone with Nick. But Sam had to grudgingly admit Nick seemed like a decent enough fellow. Though it had bothered the hell out of him to see them so close together today at lunch.

RUBY WAS UP TO HER ELBOWS in dishwater and half-way through the dinner dishes when Nick finally re-turned to the kitchen.

"That was Bailey Hardesty, the loan officer at the bank," Nick said, taking up a towel and starting to dry. "I've got to be in Rapid City for a meeting on Monday morning." He let out a frustrated sigh. "Looks like I've still got some details to hash out with the bank."

"Oh," Ruby said sympathetically. "I thought you'd finished with all that."

"Me, too," Nick said, shrugging. "Shouldn't be gone more than a day. Two at most."

Ruby handed him a plate. "And be sure to check on my new kitchen appliances while you're there. I can't wait to have a real dishwasher and a garbage disposal again."

Nick laughed as he dried. "As far as I can tell, all this old stuff works just fine. And you've been putting your scraps in the heap for compost."

Swatting him with a wet, rubber-gloved hand, Ruby scowled. "I miss having a microwave oven and a frost-free freezer. This stuff might do the job, but the other stuff will save me time and energy. I might actually have time to sit down and read a book after supper one of these days." She looked around the kitchen with its old appliances. "This might have been modern thirty years ago, but it's pretty clunky now."

Nick leaned back against the worn counter. "With

any luck, I'll be able to pick the stuff up while I'm there, and we can have your modern kitchen installed in a couple of weeks.''

"From your lips to God's ears," Ruby said. She blew a wisp of hair out of her face and pulled off her rubber gloves. "You know what? I'm giving myself tomorrow off. You've got to go to Rapid City, and Sam's moving into the apartment. I'll just have a lazy day, too. I'll go to church, maybe even catch a show at Pop's Theater. I haven't been there since he got the new projector and movie screen.''

"You've hardly been anywhere since you moved out here. I'm surprised I got you to go to Pine Run the other day," Nick said. "Just because you're going to have to come to a decision about Sam and your marriage doesn't mean you have to hide out here like a hermit.''

"I haven't been hiding like a hermit. I've been busy," Ruby said, suddenly realizing that though she hadn't intended to, she had been rather antisocial recently. "And we've gotten quite a lot accomplished, don't you think?" she added, trying to justify her secluded life.

"You still need to have a social life. You have friends in town. Go see them." Nick opened a cabinet and placed the small stack of plates on the shelf.

"I will if you take the SUV," Ruby suggested as she rinsed out the sink and turned off the water. "If the appliances are ready, you can rent a trailer and bring them back with you. Besides, I worry about you in that old truck.''

"You know I've been driving that truck since I was a teenager," Nick said. "I wouldn't know what to do without Old Betsy.''

"Well, put her in a museum, and you can visit her from time to time," Ruby said. "And take the SUV. That way I won't worry about you breaking down out in the middle of nowhere."

"I can take care of myself," Nick said, handing her the towel.

"Humor me, Nick. I'm a woman. I worry. I think it's part of the job description." Ruby swatted him with the towel. "Now, go get yourself ready for your trip to South Dakota."

"Yes, Mother," Nick said, snagging the keys to the SUV off the hook on the wall as he passed. Then he slipped out into the night.

Now that she thought about it, Ruby realized she was actually looking forward to her day in town. She knew that her friends had been worried about her, especially since she hadn't exactly acted happy after her sudden windfall. But they didn't know the entire story about Sam.

Only Honor knew that.

And Nick.

Of course, she figured by now the people of Jester had done all sorts of speculating about what was going on. Especially since Sam had shown up and had been camping out at Gwen Tanner's. Maybe it was time to shake things up.

Maybe it was time to hash things out with Sam.

Ruby sighed. All she knew was that she couldn't keep on, the way things were now. She was married, but she wasn't.

She should be happy, but she wasn't.

She loved Sam.

But she needed to be sure she could trust his word. She wanted to have a *happily-ever-after*. But the way things stood between her and Sam right now, she wasn't sure they could.

Chapter Six

Sam stood at the bottom of the outside stairway that led to the apartment over the Mercantile, a place he and Ruby had shared whenever he'd been able to get home on leave. He didn't know why he was procrastinating. It wasn't as if he'd never been there. The thing was, he realized, he'd never been there without Ruby.

Sure, he'd been alone in the apartment from time to time, but only because Ruby was downstairs or had gone out to the grocery or to visit friends. This time it was different. Ruby wouldn't be there, not because she'd be back in a little while, but because she no longer lived there. Her home was somewhere else.

Somehow, Sam found this harder to do than checking into the boardinghouse had been. He didn't like the idea of facing this place that held so many happy memories. He and Ruby had loved and laughed and planned in this humble apartment—and then everything had gone haywire.

It had all been his doing. Not Ruby's. He'd been the one to break a promise. He might have had the right reason for going out on that mission that night. After all, a combat controller never leaves a fallen teammate behind, and there had been no other man available to go on that rescue operation. Even if he hadn't been ordered to go, he would have volunteered. It had been the right thing to do.

He'd had to take that mission, but in doing it he'd screwed up big time.

Sam sucked in a deep breath and mounted the stairs. Might as well get this over with, he thought as he reached the door at the top of the stairs. He fished around in his pocket for the key and let himself in.

It was worse than he'd thought.

The living room was empty save for one lone chair—the shabby old recliner that he'd brought into the marriage. The floor had obviously been swept clean when Ruby moved out, but dust had settled in a light coating on the floor, and when he closed the door, the slight breeze caused dust motes to drift lazily into the air.

The place smelled musty and closed up, and even with the bright sun streaming in through the bare windows, the room looked barren, depressed. And that was only the living room.

Sam passed through to the bedrooms. The smaller one, the one Ruby had always hoped would house a child—their child—was as empty and barren as the living room. The floor had been swept, but here, too, a fine layer of dust coated the hardwood. There was nothing there except the broken promise of what might have been.

The other bedroom surprised him. It was if nothing had been touched. The bed was there, stripped of its covering, the queen-size mattress bare. But apparently the bedding had been washed, for it lay folded neatly at the foot of the bed. The same light coating of dust marred the surfaces of the mirrored dresser, the high chest of drawers and the night tables, but the room looked as if nothing had been disturbed.

Sam stood in the doorway wondering why Ruby had taken everything but this. Were memories of the way they had made love in this room, in that bed, too painful to remember, or too hard to forget? He hoped it was the latter. After all, they'd put that bed to good use, and he couldn't imagine anyone else sharing it, his bed, with his wife.

Pulling in a deep breath of musty air, Sam crossed to his chest of drawers and pulled one open. The civilian clothes he'd left were still there, washed and folded as if just waiting to be worn again.

He reached for the top drawer of Ruby's dresser, the one where she'd kept the lacy and delicate scraps of fabric she'd called underwear. They were empty. He yanked the rest of the drawers open. Empty as well.

Ruby had taken all of her own things, but nothing of his. It was a crystal clear commentary on how she had felt when she'd left this place to move out to the farm.

Did she still feel that way?

Ruby was his wife. And until the divorce papers were signed, sealed and delivered, he was her husband. He slammed his fist against the top of the empty dresser, disturbing the dust in the stagnant air. No. He would fight like he'd never fought before to make Ruby his again.

Other men might have given up after seeing this, but Sam was not some other man. He'd use this place to camp out in, but it would not be home. Home was where his heart was, and it wasn't here.

His heart was with Ruby.

RUBY OPENED HER EYES slowly to the bright sunlight of morning. She yawned and stretched languidly, feeling like a contented cat in front of a fire.

She didn't know how long it had been since she'd slept in past dawn. She didn't know how long it had been since she'd felt really rested.

Not since that night when—

No, she was not going to think about that now. She had the day to herself. There was nothing pressing for her to do. No chores that couldn't wait until the next morning. Petunia and the late, great Roscoe had been foraging for themselves since long before she'd taken over the farm. Petunia wouldn't notice if her morning bucket of chow came a little late. And the piglets would nuzzle up to the milk bar whether Ruby got up to feed Petunia or not.

She glanced at the clock. It was a little after eight. She could take a long, soaking bath, dress and still make it to church in plenty of time. She threw the covers aside and slid from the bed. She couldn't remember the last time she'd done more than take a quick shower, which she usually did at night, before falling into an exhausted sleep.

She glanced back at the bed, one of the few new items she'd bought when she moved to the farm. She hadn't been able to make herself bring the bed she and Sam had shared. Hadn't been able to face the thought of sleeping in it alone and knowing that Sam would never sleep with her again.

She'd deliberately chosen a different, more feminine style of furniture for this room, so there wouldn't be even a hint of Sam in it. The wood was a warm maple, and the coverings and curtains a sunny yellow.

She was comfortable in this bedroom. It was hers. No man had seen the inside of it since the new bedroom suite had been delivered. Why, then, did Sam's presence seem to haunt it?

The right side of the bed, Sam's side, was smooth and flat, the quilt barely mussed. Ruby shook her head. She still slept as if any moment she expected her husband to join her there and draw her close. She still slept as if she weren't used to sleeping alone.

And she wasn't.

Ruby knew that she'd been meant to be married. She'd been made to have children, yet no child slept under her roof. Sam had always said she could have a child anytime she wanted, but she'd put it off. She didn't want a child to grow up without a father around full-time. And Sam's job had kept him away from home far too much. She sighed and blinked back the tears that always threatened when she thought about her empty bed and her empty arms.

Now she faced growing old without Sam. And without the children she'd wanted so much.

Suddenly, her day alone, so eagerly anticipated only a few moments before, seemed like just another of a long line of lonely days to Ruby. She turned away from her startlingly empty bedroom and padded down the hall to run water in the tub.

If only filling her empty life could be as simple.

SAM MOVED his few belongings into the apartment, swept it out and had the rest of the day to kill. The hardest thing to do had been making the bed—not the physical task, but thinking about the reason Ruby must have had for stripping it bare. Had she been so angry with him that she couldn't bear for anything that had once touched his body to touch her again?

He threw open the windows to let the balmy spring air into the apartment. As it swirled through, clearing the musty, dank odor away, it did nothing to expunge the regrets and memories from Sam's heart. He wandered from room to room, aimless and lost, wondering what he could do to make this place seem more like a home. Nothing came to mind.

There was only one thing, one person who could make this place a home. Ruby.

And he knew she wouldn't come.

His stomach grumbled, and Sam realized he would have to find something to eat. On a Sunday in Jester, that would prove a problem. He'd eaten breakfast at Gwen's, but the Brimming Cup was closed on Sundays, as was the grocery store. He guessed he'd have to make the trip to Pine Run for a few supplies to hold him until he could figure out how to make Ruby want him again.

He closed the windows, made a quick mental list of what he needed, then loped down the outside stairs. He stopped short at the bottom, nearly colliding with Ruby, who appeared to be stopping by to check on the store.

She raised her hand to her mouth to stifle a gasp, and stared at him for a moment, giving Sam a chance to look at her, as well. She was wearing a dress in a slightly old-fashioned, high-collared style, but she still looked damned hot. This was the first time he'd seen her hair down since he'd been back in Jester, and Sam longed to run his hands through those fiery waves. Even at arm's length she made his groin tighten.

"You startled me," Ruby finally said.

"I'm sorry." But Sam wasn't sorry one bit. After all, any time he caught Ruby off her guard gave him a chance to work his way back into her affections. "I didn't expect to find you here, either." Not that it wasn't a pleasant surprise, but he didn't say that out loud.

"Are you going somewhere?"

"Yeah. To Pine Run for supplies. I forgot that everything in Jester closes on Sundays." Sam hated the way they were standing at arm's length like a couple of strangers, making idle conversation about nothing in particular. He had a sudden stroke of inspiration. "Want to go with me? You've been cooking for me this week. How 'bout I treat you to Sunday dinner?" Especially since Nick appeared to be nowhere around. Any time Sam got a chance to be alone with his wife, he'd take it.

Ruby opened her mouth to speak, then closed it again quickly, and Sam knew better than to press. They might be acting like strangers, but they weren't. And he knew that if he pushed too hard, his stubborn, redheaded wife would balk like an ornery mule. She looked at him, her emerald eyes wide, and gnawed at her lip with indecision. After what seemed like an eternity, she swallowed hard and answered. "Yes, thank you. I'd like that."

"Hoo-ah!" Sam said softly, using the traditional airborne expression for hurrah, and was pleased to note that Ruby's mouth twitched as she tried to suppress a smile. He crooked an arm, and after only a slight hesitation, Ruby looped hers through it. A thousand volts of awareness seemed to charge through him as he escorted Ruby to the car.

Only then did Sam realize that Ruby had apparently arrived in Nick's truck. Her new SUV was nowhere in sight. A wave of disappointment dimmed the electricity between them. "You came with Nick?" he said, trying to temper the disappointment in his voice.

Ruby looked up quickly. "Oh, no. Nick's gone to Rapid City for a few days to take care of some business. I let him take my car. He might love this rattle-trap of his, but I shudder to think about what would happen if he broke down out in the middle of nowhere."

Sam pushed aside a couple of uncharitable thoughts about Nick staying lost in the middle of nowhere, and decided to simply be glad that Nick's absence gave him the opportunity to try to get back in his wife's good graces. And her bed, if he was lucky. "Too bad," he said insincerely. Then he steered Ruby toward the Corvette.

"THAT WAS GOOD," Ruby said, pushing the remains of a decadent chocolate dessert away from her. "But I couldn't eat another bite." She wouldn't have ordered the rich dessert, but Sam had always known about her sweet tooth and he'd ordered it for her. Over some very weak protests, she had to admit.

"You mind if I polish off the rest?" he asked, reaching for the dish.

Ruby laughed. "I don't know where you'll put it. You already ate one of your own, and you want mine, too?"

"Hey, you work me hard on that farm, woman," Sam growled as he forked up a generous mouthful of chocolate.

"You asked for it," Ruby said. "I was never one to turn down free help. Just ask Nick."

Sam's cheerful expression disappeared as fast as the cake. Why he was so touchy about Nick she didn't know, but it gave Ruby a small measure of satisfaction that Nick's presence bothered him.

"It's nice to see how much weight you've put on since I've been 'working you,'" Ruby commented as Sam scarfed down the chocolate dessert. "It looks good on you."

Sam's cheerful expression returned as he finished the cake.

Ruby plucked her napkin up off her lap and laid it on the table. "Come on," she said. "Let's go. You still have shopping to do. I know all too well that if I left you to your own devices you'd buy nothing but corn chips and chocolate brownies."

"Aw, honey," Sam said, grinning. "You have to know I'd throw in some fried pork skins and maybe a couple of apples to balance it all out."

"Exactly," Ruby said primly. "That's why I have to save you from yourself."

"You know me too well," Sam said, pushing his chair back. "Let's go," he said, offering her his arm again.

Ruby accepted and fought to push back the delicious tingles of anticipation as she rested her hand on his arm. She had to learn not to go all tingly at his touch, she reminded herself as they waited in line at the cash register.

She forced herself to think about something other than Sam. Dinner had been pleasant, though slightly strained, she thought, as she waited while Sam paid the check. Though the green beans had been overcooked and the pot roast stringy, she'd still enjoyed it. It was seldom that she got to eat a meal someone else prepared, and in the last week, she'd eaten out three times: once in the company of Nick, once with Sam and once with both men. How odd, she thought, that she would feel more comfortable with Nick than with her own husband, the man she'd been married to for ten years.

She was well aware that Sam wanted her back. She was also aware of the sexual energy that seemed to be zinging between them, but she couldn't forget the magnitude of Sam's betrayal. Until she was certain she could trust him with her heart, she would not trust him with her body. She knew all too well how easy it would be to fall into the same old routine. How simple it would be to let Sam take her and kiss her and hold her and make lo—

No, she had to stop that. She had to be strong. Until she was sure that Sam would stay, she would not let him back into her heart.

"Ready to go?" he asked, bringing Ruby out of her thoughts.

"The Super Store on the main highway is probably the only place open this afternoon," she said. "This isn't the big city, either, even if it is bigger than Jester."

"The Super Store it is, then," Sam said agreeably. He crooked his arm, and Ruby took it and allowed him to escort her out to the car. This time it was a little easier to squelch the gooey feeling she got when he touched her. And she almost wished it hadn't been.

As he opened the car door for her, Sam was every bit the gentleman he'd been when she'd first met him eleven years ago. He held her hand, and Ruby slipped inside. As much as she hated this fast car, she enjoyed the looks that people gave them whenever they were out in it. She knew that she and Sam made a striking couple. Sam with his well-trimmed dark hair, military bearing and steely-gray eyes hidden behind the aviator-style sunglasses, and she with her eye-catching red hair never failed to turn heads. And in spite of everything that had passed between them, Ruby had to admit she liked the notion that they still looked so good together.

Sam started the engine and drove off, and while he was concentrating on his driving, Ruby took the opportunity to look at him, really look at him. The few days he had been working on the farm in the fresh air and sun had replaced his pallor with the beginnings of a healthy tan. His injured leg seemed stronger already. Apparently, all those meals she'd cooked for him were making a difference, too. Not to mention half of her dessert today.

Ruby smiled as she leaned back in the seat, remembering the way he had hungrily cleaned his plate and asked for seconds, then looked at her just as hungrily. She knew that part of it had been from appetite, but she also knew that it had been a ploy to stay with her, if only for a few moments longer. A ploy she had tolerated, but not really encouraged.

She still didn't know what to make of Sam's sudden reappearance after staying away for so long. Her smile faded. If he wanted her so badly, why hadn't he come back sooner? Why had he reappeared just when she thought she might have finally begun to get him out of her system?

She glanced again at Sam as he drove. Would he leave her once he became strong enough to do so?

Ruby gnawed at her lip, a habit from childhood she'd never been able to break. As much as Sam Cade had let her down, she still needed him. She still loved him, and she wanted him to stay with her forever.

She just hoped that if he was going to let her down, he'd do it now, before it was too late. Before she'd gotten used to having him around again. Before she'd had a chance to depend on him, to want him again. As if she'd ever stopped.

She'd learned that she could live without him, or at least survive. But as hard as she'd tried, she'd also learned that she didn't want to. She didn't know many single men in and around Jester, Montana, but the few she did know could not compare to Captain Samuel Cade, USAF Retired.

As Sam eased the car into the parking lot in front of the giant Super Store, all Ruby could think of was how she might get her husband back and how she could do so without losing face. Without giving up all that she'd strived to achieve since they'd been separated. Since she'd thought she'd be able to make it on her own...

And realized she couldn't.

THERE WAS STILL A LOT of day left, but Sam couldn't think of any more reasons to stay in Pine Run with Ruby. And the TV dinners he'd bought at the Super Store would defrost. Not that he cared.

Not if it meant he'd have a few more minutes alone with his wife.

"Well, I guess we'd better get your purchases back to Jester and in the refrigerator before they spoil," Ruby said, her practical streak showing a mile wide.

Sam let out a long, low breath as he stashed the

last of the bags in the Corvette's small trunk and closed it. "I reckon we should," he replied sourly. He forced himself to flash a smile in Ruby's direction as he opened the passenger door for her. "Get in."

She did, with just a little too much alacrity to suit Sam.

As he closed the door and walked around to the driver's side, he grinned to himself. He didn't have to drive his normal racing-car speed when he hit the highway. She'd see right through his intentions if he poked along at thirty or forty miles an hour, but if he drove at a modest sixty-five, what could she say? And that would prolong the trip some. Maybe when they reached Jester, he could convince Ruby to come up and help him put the stuff away.

It was worth a try.

He settled in the cockpit of his low-flying craft, positioned his aviator glasses on his face and turned the key. As the powerful engine roared to life, he let the pressure off the accelerator. Then he eased out of the parking spot and out onto Route 2 back toward Jester.

Sam cast a sideways glance at Ruby and saw that she had clutched the armrests of the bucket seat as though she were preparing for a takeoff at two or three g's. Her full lips were pressed together with tension, but when it became apparent that he wasn't going to fly along the highway at his usual breakneck speed, she seemed to relax slightly. Sam couldn't help smiling to himself.

Ruby sighed softly, and he knew it was because she was relieved not to feel the car accelerate beneath her. If this was all it took to please her, he could have done it a long time ago, but he knew that their problems went deeper than the speed at which he drove. He wondered if he should say anything, but he didn't really know what to talk about. Maybe the break in the silence should come from Ruby, not from him.

They'd driven about five miles before she finally spoke. "Is there some reason you're driving so slowly?" she finally asked.

Sam grinned. Ruby had noticed. "Well," he drawled, "I have precious cargo on board," he said. "You."

He cast another quick glance toward Ruby and saw that her alabaster skin had flushed to a shade that matched her name. He had gotten her attention with that one. She lifted one small hand to her throat and held it there. Her lips opened as if she wanted to speak, but all she said was, "Oh."

But Sam knew he'd made Ruby think. He liked that he'd caught her off guard with that comment. He reached over and placed his hand on hers, which was still on the armrest, and squeezed gently. It pleased him no end when she didn't pull away.

Ruby let him hold her hand like that all the way back to Jester.

And when he had to let go so that he could downshift at the town limits, she uttered a brief whimper of protest that warmed him all the way down to his toes.

Sam wished he could keep her there, captive in his car, his hand covering hers, until Ruby begged him to stay. But he knew that he had to take this slowly, even if his body was clamoring for immediate action.

He eased the car into its space behind the store. Ruby let out a soft sigh, which Sam tried to read. Was it because she was relieved that she'd gotten home in one piece in spite of him practically making the car crawl home, or was it because she was sad that the ride had ended?

When he hurried around and helped her out, she accepted his hand, and he loved the way her fingers felt, so soft and warm in his. But once she was out of the car, she withdrew her hand, wiped it nervously on her skirt and stood straight. She seemed to have something on her mind, and Sam hoped it was him.

"I need to check inventory in the Mercantile," she said, fishing in her purse for the key. "I've been leaving too much to Honor and the rest of the staff since I've been out on the farm," she said by way of explanation. "You don't mind if I don't help you with your groceries, do you?"

Sam did mind, but he knew he shouldn't push even though he wanted to. No, he wanted to pick her up, sweep her off her feet, toss her over his shoulder and carry her up to that big bed upstairs. That's what he wanted to do, but he swallowed his desire and forced a smile. "No. I wondered who was taking care of the store while you were out there at the farm."

"Honor's been keeping things going. And the place pretty much runs itself, anyway, with a couple of employees who've been here longer than I have," Ruby said, a relieved look on her face. "Still, I should do my share. Honor wanted me to look things over. She's thinking about going away for a while."

"I guess she deserves a vacation as much as anybody else," Sam said, disappointed that Ruby wouldn't be giving him a chance to try to get her into his bed. He had a feeling that if they could just once make love, it would break the awful tension that stretched so tightly between them.

"Well," Ruby said, sounding breathless and nervous and…what? "I'd best get started. It's late and…"

Sam didn't know why he did it, but he just couldn't seem to help himself. They were standing at the back door of the Mercantile, as nervous and jumpy as a couple of teenagers at a girl's front door after their first date. It was more instinct than plan, but Sam simply reacted.

He reached for Ruby, pulled her to him and pressed her body against his. He could feel her heart fluttering against her rib cage like a captive bird, but nothing was going to stop him now that he had gone this far.

Ruby stared up at him, her green eyes wide, her lips slightly parted in question. Sam lowered his head and Ruby's lids drifted downward. He captured her lips.

She didn't pull away.

Ruby felt her arms go up around Sam's neck as though they had a will of their own. She hadn't consciously wanted to respond to Sam's kiss; in fact, when she'd learned he was back in town, she'd vowed not to let him kiss her. But she seemed helpless to resist.

Warmth flooded through her blood from her head to her toes and her skin tingled with delight as she felt her body go aching and tender and soft. Her lips parted, and she let Sam's searching tongue in. She responded to him in kind, to this dance of tongues, this unspoken communication of their bodies, their minds. Their heartbeats seemed to pound in tandem, their every movement came together in a rhythm that was old as time. Ruby found herself completely under Sam's spell.

Which was why she wrenched herself painfully free of his arms. She couldn't think clearly—no, she couldn't think at all—with Sam doing this to her.

She backed safely away from him, her breasts rising and falling as she tried to catch her breath. Her pulse raced, and her heart beat so loudly she could barely hear herself think. "No, Sam," she finally blurted out. "I can't allow this to happen. Not yet. Not again. We have too many issues to discuss, too many differences to work out before I can let myself go with you."

To Sam's credit, he didn't protest. He stepped back, a maddening, knowing smile on his lips. She ought to be angry with him, but how could she when she loved the man with all her heart? But love notwithstanding, she couldn't bear to have her heart broken again. Not when it was still not completely healed.

Sam stepped back, too, his arms raised in silent surrender. "I won't say I'm sorry I kissed you, Ruby, because I'm not. But I am sorry I hurt you and made you feel this way." He stepped back another couple of steps, until he was against the redbrick wall of the store. "Believe me when I tell you I intend to do everything I possibly can to make you trust that our marriage will work, and that this time I'm going to stay."

He brushed past her, opened the truck of the car, removed his packages and hurried up the steps, his right leg dragging slightly as he went.

Ruby didn't know what to think. Here she was, standing in the back alley behind the store, and she didn't know what to do. Her husband had told her he wanted her back, yet she was still reluctant to believe him. What if his leg healed and he regained his strength? Already, in just the few days he'd been helping out at the farm, he looked better, stronger.

What if he couldn't take the simple, boring life that she looked forward to on the farm? What if somebody came along and offered him more excitement? Would he want it more than he wanted her?

Only time would tell.

And Ruby felt as though she had no time. She wanted the answers today, this minute, not six months or six years in the future. Yes, she believed that Sam meant what he said when he told her he loved her and wanted to spend the rest of his life with her. Today.

But what about tomorrow?

She let out a long, deep sigh, reached into her purse for her keys and let herself into the store.

She needed something normal, familiar, to ground her. And the store was there. Maybe if she could just get herself into some sort of routine she could start to think straight again.

She shut the door and reached for the switch. As the room flooded with light, she knew one thing: coming to a conclusion about what to do with Sam was not going to be as simple as switching on a light.

The old attraction was still there. Even if it had been more than a year since Sam had held her in his arms, she still felt as though she belonged there. She loved him. She wanted him. She longed to stay in his arms forever. She wanted him to take her to bed and love her.

But she was still not certain he wouldn't leave her again. She wouldn't trade a few moments of pleasure for a lifetime of heartbreak. It had taken her this long to even begin to get over Sam. She would not go through it again.

Chapter Seven

Sam let himself into the apartment, closed the door behind him and dropped his parcels on the kitchen counter. Then he let loose with an exultant "Hooah!" He cheered again and grinned with satisfaction.

He might not have managed to seduce Ruby back into his bed today, but he had learned something that was almost as good. Ruby's feelings for him were still as strong as ever. The way she'd responded to his kiss proved that. And the way she'd pushed herself away so abruptly. She still loved him, wanted him, desired him, but she didn't want to.

That he could fix.

Or so he hoped.

He didn't have to make her love him all over again. She still did. All he had to do was make her *want* to love him.

And he was afraid that would be more of a challenge than actually getting back into her bed.

But he was a combat controller—a special operations combat controller, at that. He might no longer wear the uniform, his leg might not work the same as it had, but he was still the same inside. And a combat controller never backed down from a challenge.

Ruby might have tried to get him out of her life, but he'd seen plain as day that she really didn't want to. Not deep inside where it mattered.

His wife still loved him as much as he loved her.

Now all he had to do was make her want him in her life again.

"Hoo-ah!" he cheered again, drew in his stomach and pushed his chest out, big and wide. "I can do this," he told himself, pounding on his chest with his fist. "Yes sir, I can do this."

He glanced at the pile of unpacked grocery sacks. He figured he had enough supplies to last about a week. He whistled confidently as he began to put the stuff away. "One week," he said to himself. "That ought to do it. One more week and Ruby will be mine again."

He figured he could hold out that long.

"Hoo-ah!"

RUBY SAT at the scarred rolltop desk and stared off into space. What had just happened between her and Sam? Had it been a momentary lapse, or had it been a near surrender in a battle of wills? She had to harden her heart against Sam or she'd never be able to think clearly about him. She had to stop turning to melted marshmallows whenever he got close.

Trouble was, she liked the way she felt when Sam touched her. She liked the way she felt in Sam's arms. No, she didn't just like it, she loved it. And she loved Sam.

Whether she wanted to or not.

"No. Stop this, Ruby Cade," she told herself. "You're not sitting in this office to think about Sam.

You have a store to attend to, and thinking about what might be is no way to get the work done.''

She logged on to the store's computer and forced herself to get started.

Ruby managed to go over the accounts, but it wasn't easy. Every time she heard a board creak or the sound of Sam's footsteps in the apartment above her, she was reminded of how close he was. Though he wasn't in the small office, she felt his presence there as though he were.

Finally, she gave up and turned off the computer. Honor had kept the books in perfect shape, so there wasn't that much to do, and Ruby did have a long drive back to the farm. And tomorrow morning would come early as ever.

Even if she had taken the day off.

Especially since she'd taken the day off.

There would be twice as much to do, and she was expecting Melinda Hartman to come out to check on the piglets. Ruby had to smile. The piglets were so cute. And one of them had even started following her around like a puppy. How could anyone send anything so adorable off to slaughter?

Ruby let out a long, low sigh, then started to tidy up the office. With the lottery win, both she and Honor had been distracted from operations of the business. But fortunately, their well-trained employees practically ran the place. Still, she really would have to spend more time on the business, even if it meant less time at the farm.

At least she had Sam there to give her a hand, especially now that Nick seemed so close to getting his loan and going back to Rapid City to start his construction firm. He wouldn't be around much longer to help her out.

She stepped out onto the back stoop and shook her head. Why couldn't she just keep Sam out of the picture?

THE NEXT DAY, Ruby turned down the gas under the skillet full of sausage and glanced at the clock on the wall above the stove. It was almost eight o'clock and Sam had not yet arrived. It wasn't like him to be late, nor was it like him to back out on a promise, and he had promised to be here to help out while Nick was gone.

Had he taken her rejection of him yesterday as a reason to give up on her?

No. She shook her head. There had to be a good reason. And Sam would explain.

As soon as he got here.

If he was really coming.

Ruby scooped the sausage up with a spatula and laid the patties on a plate lined with paper towels to drain. Why did she have so many doubts about Sam?

After so many months of trying to get him out of her system, why was she upset that he might actually be going?

She cracked an egg against the side of a mixing bowl with so much force that the shell broke and yolk went everywhere.

"Doggone it. This is all I need," she muttered as she grabbed paper towels to clean up the mess. "I hope I don't have to mop the floor."

Ruby managed to get the sticky yellow stuff off the worn linoleum with a sponge. As she rinsed it for the second time, she muttered, "Where the heck is that man when I need him?"

"Well, darlin'. I didn't know you still cared."

Ruby spun around, slipping on the wet spot and all but falling into Sam's arms. He dropped a newspaper tucked under his arm and adroitly caught her and held her upper arms, caressing them, running his fingers lightly up and down her sleeves.

"I didn't hear you drive up, what with the water running," Ruby said lamely as Sam's arms tightened around her. Little tingles of excitement and desire skittered up and down her arms, but she forced herself to step back.

"Aw, come on, sugar. I thought you missed me," Sam said cheerfully. He grinned and let her go.

"Just your body," Ruby said, and instantly regretted it.

"Hoo-ah! Sounding better and better," Sam cheered.

Ruby rolled her eyes. "Give me a break, Sam," she said. "I need your body to work. Nothing more. I took yesterday off, so we're already behind. You're late, and Dr. Hartman's coming to check on Petunia and the piglets this afternoon. We have to go round them up. What kept you, anyway?"

"Picked up a newspaper." Sam stood unnervingly close to Ruby, and her breath caught in her throat as he reached behind her into the cupboard for plates and a mug. "Oh, and while I'm thinking about it... What do you know about the pavilion falling down?"

"Not much," Ruby said as she cracked another egg, more gently this time, into the mixing bowl. "It was during the Founders' Day Celebration. Melinda Woods—Hartman now—got beaned on the head when it collapsed. I thought it was because of snow buildup on the roof, but Luke had an engineer come out and look at it, and he confirmed that it had been tampered with.'' She cracked two more eggs in quick succession and started whipping them with a fork. "Why are you asking?"

Sam shrugged. "The sheriff asked me to do some nosing around to see if I could find out anything."

"You? Why you?"

He stepped back and scooped up the newspaper. "He thought I might be able to use some of my covert operative skills to learn something."

Ruby arched an eyebrow. "Makes sense. You don't know that many people in town." She put down the fork and looked up. "Oh, and Melinda's coming over this afternoon to show me how to deworm the piglets. Maybe you can ask her about it then."

Sam poured his coffee and took a swig. He watched her over the rim of his mug, and Ruby felt a shiver of—what? Excitement? Annoyance? "I just might do that," he said, leaning casually against the counter and watching as she tried to concentrate on cooking. "Did you know that someone tried to burn it?"

"What? The pavilion? Why?"

"Beats me." Sam shrugged. "Why does anybody do stupid things like that?"

Ruby poured the beaten eggs into the skillet and listened to the satisfying sizzle as the eggs hit the hot pan. "Well, our illustrious mayor, Bobby Larson, has been talking about putting up a big hotel on the parkland to lure more business into town. I'm not sure he can do that, though, since the property belongs to the community."

"But if the pavilion were out of the way, it would

be easier to convince his constituents to replace it with a hotel," Sam said thoughtfully.

"I don't think so, Sam," Ruby said, grabbing a potholder and scooping the eggs out of the frying pan and onto plates. "Bobby's ambitious, but he's not stupid. Surely he wouldn't take such drastic measures. There's no sense in speculating until you have some evidence. Besides, I think maybe Bobby's abandoned that idea, since so many people were against it."

"Why?" Sam took the plate of sausage and his coffee to the table and sat down. "I would think that a big new hotel would bring lots of new business to Jester. It isn't exactly thriving, you know."

Ruby nodded. "Too many people were afraid it would ruin it. You know, take away the friendly, small-town atmosphere." She set one of the plates of eggs in front of Sam and joined him at the table, removing the cloth covering a bowl of biscuits as she sat. "Eat up. We have to get to work. We need to finish repairing the pigpen before Melinda comes."

"Still, it's something to think about," Sam said, opening the paper and glancing inside. He muttered a curse.

"What?"

"Oh, hell," Sam said grimly. "There's something about us in the 'Neighborly Nuggets from Jester' gossip column. I wonder if we can sue?"

"What? Are you sure it's about us?" she asked, reaching for the paper.

Sam jerked it away. "Listen to this. 'A certain separated millionaire was seen having a cozy lunch with her hired hand in Pine Run the other day. Two days later, that same millionaire was seen out and about with her estranged hubby. What's up? Could she be having her cake and eating it, too?'" Sam slammed the pages together and crumpled the paper into a tight ball.

Ruby sat there, too shocked for a moment to speak. Finally, she said, "Why would anybody say such an awful thing?"

"Jealousy," Sam muttered. "Nothing but spite and jealousy." He tossed the balled paper toward the trash can. "But that's okay, because I'll find out who did this and I'll make them regret it. Hell, I'll make 'em regret they were ever born."

SAM TURNED UP HIS COLLAR against the damp, northerly breeze brought in by a late-season cold front during the night, and strode across the farmyard toward the shed where they'd penned up Petunia and the piglets. Dr. Hartman was due to arrive any minute, and he was glad he wouldn't have to round up the pigs when she did.

Odd that he hadn't even noticed the pigs until Ruby mentioned the tale of Petunia and Roscoe the other day. But now Sam understood why. Petunia and the piglets had pretty much free run of the land between the house and the creek, and since they hadn't been fed regularly, Petunia apparently saw no reason to venture close to the house. In the balmy weather of the past few days, she'd enjoyed resting in the shade of the trees near the creek. But now, with a storm front moving through and drastically lower temperatures, it was warmer in the hog shed. Petunia was content to shelter her family from the elements, lying in fresh, clean straw.

He had a couple more rails to nail into place and the hog pen would be secure. Although the piglets could easily slip under the rails, he supposed they would stay close to their mother until they were too big to escape. A guy could hope, anyway.

Nick had left the boards lying on the ground near the fence, and all Sam had to do was knock them into place. He pulled a nail out of his pocket with his left hand and hefted the hammer in his right. This ought to be a snap.

He lifted a board—it was heavier than he'd expected—and positioned it against the support post, bracing it with his leg. Then he placed the nail and whammed it.

The hammer slipped and Sam dropped the rail, narrowly missing his foot. He positioned the board again, this time giving the nail a gentle tap the first time, to hold it in place. It slipped again, and he pounded his thumb.

Sam muttered a pungent curse, dropped the hammer, then stuck his thumb in his mouth to ease the pain. Nick had made it look so simple. Apparently, this wasn't as easy as it appeared. Sam took his thumb out of his mouth, shook it to ease the throbbing, and let out a long sigh. If he kept this up, all his fingers were going to be black and blue.

He had to hand it to Nick. The man did know what he was doing.

And Sam was well out of his element here. What the hell was he doing, trying to make a go of a farm? He knew more about nuclear physics than he did farming. And he knew damn little about nuclear physics.

''Need some help?''

Grateful that his back was to Ruby, Sam jerked his aching thumb out of his mouth. ''Yeah,'' he said.

"Can you hold this rail in place so I can nail? The wood's wet and it keeps slipping."

"Sure," Ruby said, stepping up behind him. "I helped Nick do this the other day."

"Good to know that Nick can't do everything by himself," Sam muttered sourly.

"What was that?"

"Nothing," he lied. "Just do whatever you did with Nick and let's get this done before the vet gets here." He didn't even want to think what she might have been doing with Nick.

Ruby picked up the board with gloved hands and held it in place, bracing herself against it with one leg. Sam quickly set the nail. "Thanks," he said. "With your help we'll have this done in no time."

Even with the distraction of Ruby being close by, Sam got the fence rails nailed on in short order. He stepped back and surveyed his work. "Not bad, for an amateur," he said.

Ruby cocked an eyebrow, but said nothing.

"Feel free to heap praise on me any time now, sugar," he prodded.

"It looks fine, Sam," Ruby said. "It's a fence, not the Taj Mahal."

Sam started to take exception to Ruby's remark, but he was stopped by the sound of a car horn. He looked up to see a white, four-wheel-drive truck pull up. Emblazoned on the doors were the words…Jester Veterinary Clinic.

"That's Melinda," Ruby said, waving and starting toward her. "Looks like we got done just in time."

A small woman with dark blond hair stepped out of the truck. She waved and reached inside for something.

"That's the vet? She doesn't look like she could lift a toy poodle, much less Petunia."

Ruby made a face. "She doesn't need to bench-press three hundred pounds to do this job. She uses her brain, not brawn."

Sam shrugged and stuck his hands in his pockets. "Whatever." At least he'd be there to offer assistance. But only if asked.

"How are the little darlings?" Melinda called, carrying what looked like an old-fashioned doctor's bag.

"Fat and happy and growing like weeds," Ruby answered. "And they're, conveniently for us, waiting in the hog shed."

"Good," the vet said. "Then this'll only take a few minutes." She turned to Sam and offered her hand. "Hi, I'm Melinda Woods Hartman."

"Sam Cade," he said, accepting it. Her grip was strong and firm. Maybe she could do this job. "Anything I can do to help, I'm here."

Ruby pulled open the shed door and, as they stepped inside, Melinda drew an apple from her pocket. As soon as Petunia saw it, she lumbered to her feet with a friendly grunt and ambled over to the vet.

"That's a good girl," Melinda said, putting her bag down on the floor and giving the pig the apple. She gave her a quick examination, then turned to Ruby. "She looks good. Augmenting what she can root up on her own really makes a difference, doesn't it, sweetie?" she said to the pig, rubbing her under the chin and murmuring baby talk to the animal. "You're such a good girl. Now, let's look at your babies."

The piglets, which had been huddled close to Petunia when they came in, were now on their feet and watching their mother and Melinda curiously. Sam had to admit they were cute.

"This shouldn't be too hard," Melinda said, picking up her bag. She undid the clasp and pulled out a large, clear, hollow syringe. "The medicine is sweet. Once they taste it, they gobble it right down."

"Oh, it's not a shot then?" Sam said, eyeing the syringe. Maybe this would be a piece of cake.

"Nope. We just squeeze it in. Easy as pie."

With Sam catching the piglets, Ruby holding them and Melinda administering the sticky yellow syrup, the first three performed as Melinda had promised. The fourth and final piglet, one Ruby had dubbed Oscar, apparently had other ideas.

As Sam reached for him, Oscar darted away between Sam's legs and out the shed door in a break for freedom. Sam started after him as Oscar scampered across the yard, through puddles and mud. Damn, that pig could move!

Too bad he couldn't move as fast.

He thought he had Oscar cornered by one of the cold frames, but the piglet feinted and dodged, darting away. Sam turned to follow and slipped in the mud. He tried to right himself, but his bad leg went out from under him with a searing flash of pain, and he landed soundly on his backside in a puddle. Oscar paused and watched, seeming to enjoy the spectacle as Sam tried to catch his breath. Was the blasted animal actually laughing at him?

Sam muttered a curse and scrambled to his feet, unsuccessfully scrabbling for purchase in the clinging mud. Just as he reached the pig, Oscar turned and headed for the wide-open spaces near the creek.

Dripping mud, Sam shook himself off, then hurried

after him. Melinda and Ruby joined the chase, and the three of them managed to capture the fleeing piglet before he made a clean getaway.

"Do not say a single word!" Sam growled as they trudged back to the hog shed.

Ruby tried to stifle her giggles, but Sam did look ridiculous, covered in mud and who knew what else, as he held the squirming, squealing piglet against his chest in a death grip. "I can't help it, Sam. You look like the Creature from the Black Lagoon."

He growled.

Even Melinda looked amused, though it was apparent she was trying hard not to laugh. "I'm sorry, Sam. That does happen sometimes. It comes with the territory."

Sam grunted. "Let's just get it over with or I might just make this…this creature into pork chops," he muttered as they reached the hog shed.

Melinda reached into her case for another syringe, measured out the correct amount of medicine and quickly administered the dose.

Job done, Sam carried the squalling piglet to the newly finished pen, lifted him over the rails and let him loose. The animal shook himself and scampered indignantly away, ducking under the fence rail on the opposite side of the pen. He stood just outside the enclosure, seeming to taunt them.

Sam glared, but Ruby caught him by the arm. "Oscar's okay. He can't get into anything right now."

"And in a few weeks he'll be too big to go under the rails." Melinda closed her case and smiled. "Well, that's done. I hate to dose and run, but I still have to get out to the Purcell place this afternoon.

Maybe I'll have time for coffee next time, Ruby."
She picked up the case and strode out to her truck.

"Anytime, Melinda. See you," Ruby said, waving.
Then she turned back to Sam.

"Don't even think about laughing, Ruby," Sam
said through gritted teeth as he tried to brush the
thick, clinging muck and mud off his pants.

"Oh, I wouldn't dream of it," Ruby said, again
trying to stifle her mirth. But her attempts were less
than successful, and she burst into gales of laughter.
"I don't know what was funnier—watching you run
after that runaway piggy or seeing you try to get up
out of that muddy puddle," she said when she finally
regained control.

Sam looked as though he was trying to maintain a
stern expression, but Ruby could see the twinkle in
his eyes. Soon he was laughing, too.

It felt so good to laugh again.

To be laughing with Sam.

"Seriously, though," Sam said once they'd gotten
past their laughter. "I've got to drive back to town in
these pants. I have a clean shirt here, but I don't have
a complete change of clothes. If I had an old farm
truck, it wouldn't be a big deal, but I've got—" He
stopped abruptly, as if he realized he was putting too
much emphasis on a material possession like an
eleven-year-old sports car.

"But you don't want to ruin the seats in the Corvette," Ruby finished for him.

"Something like that," Sam agreed. "Do you have
some old sheets or towels I can put on the seat?"

"No, I bought all new. But why don't you just give
me the jeans, and I'll run them through the washer

and dryer? You can shower and they'll be washing and drying while we eat.''

"Works for me," Sam said. "Are we done for the day?"

"There's nothing that can't wait till tomorrow. You can shower off while I feed Petunia. I'll get your wet stuff when I'm finished."

"Yes, ma'am," Sam said, saluting. Then he pivoted and marched toward the house.

Appreciating the view of his backside in the damp and clinging jeans, Ruby chuckled as she watched Sam go. His limp was barely noticeable these days. Or had she just gotten so used to seeing it that she no longer noticed?

Ruby dumped feed into Petunia's trough. Though the sow had been fending for herself in the wild, she seemed to welcome the food, and she had apparently learned to anticipate feeding time. Ruby knew these animals were not pets like potbellied pigs, but still, she couldn't bear the thought of sending them off to be somebody's Sunday pork roast. Not after she'd met them face-to-face.

"You know something, Petunia? You and your children are one lucky family. What do you think of that?"

Petunia didn't reply, so Ruby turned and trudged back to the house.

She could hear water running in the shower as soon as she entered. Sam had left the door open to let the steam out so he could see in the mirror to shave, something he'd always done when they were married.

What was she thinking? They were still married. Technically, anyway.

As Ruby hurried to the bathroom, the water

stopped running. "Do you need a towel?" she called as she moved down the hall. "I'll just get your wet things and leave you alone," she said, bustling into the room. But Sam had already stepped out from behind the curtain.

True, he had wrapped a towel modestly around his waist, but the sight of her husband, half-naked from the shower, was not what shocked her. The angry-looking mass of scar tissue that covered his leg from ankle to thigh did.

Ruby gasped, unable to draw her gaze away from Sam's mangled leg. "Why didn't you tell me it was this bad?" she finally managed to ask, her voice barely above a whisper.

Sam shrugged. "I didn't think you'd care."

Ruby covered her mouth with her hand and forced her gaze away from Sam's injuries. Tears welled in her eyes, and she tried to blink them back. "Of course I care, Sam. I've always cared," she said, choking back a sob. "I cared too much. Don't you realize that every time you went off on a mission I held my breath until you came back to me safe and sound? I hung on to every report, every fragment of news, hoping for some tiny bit of information about how you were doing. Some clue that you were all right. Every time I thought about the possibility of you dying and leaving me alone, I died a little bit myself. I just couldn't take it anymore." Ruby turned away, chagrined that she had confessed so much to him.

"I wish you'd have told me that a long time ago, Ruby," Sam said huskily.

"I was afraid if you were worried about me, you wouldn't have your mind completely on your job, and it would cause you to make a mistake."

"And there I was fine and happy, thinking that you were safe at home, and instead you were worrying yourself to death. You should have told me, Ruby. It might have made a difference." He reached for her and tipped her face up to his.

"Would it?"

"I don't know," he said, looking into Ruby's eyes. The expression in his gray ones mirrored his confusion as well as her own. "I'd like to think it might have."

"I'm sorry, Sam. I really am." Tears coursed down Ruby's cheeks, unchecked. "I didn't know."

Sam cupped her face with one hand, then brushed the tears away with the tip of his thumb. "I'm sorry, too," he murmured. Then he kissed her lightly on the lips and let go.

When she turned away, he called her back. "Ruby?"

She looked back quickly. "Yes?"

"It happened, Ruby. We can't undo it."

She drew in a deep breath. "How did it happen?" she asked expectantly, hoping that the full story would lift some of the blame off her shoulders.

Chapter Eight

"There's not much to tell," Sam said simply, staring off into space. He couldn't look at her, not right now. He didn't want Ruby to see the pain in his eyes. This wasn't exactly the way he had planned this, standing there in the bathroom, wrapped in a towel, but he might as well get it over with.

"I got back from that mission a couple days later, and I heard you'd called. You never called in the middle of the week, so I was worried. I was afraid something bad had happened. And when Honor answered, it seemed to confirm my worst fears.

"Then she started babbling about winning the lottery, and I finally figured out that was probably what you'd called about. I asked to talk to you, and Honor said you wouldn't talk to me. I figured maybe I'd misunderstood and you were busy in the store, so I asked Honor to tell you to call me back.

"She seemed pretty uncomfortable, but she said she would give you the message." He drew in a deep shuddering breath, then went on. "I waited for you to call, but you didn't, so I called you and called you, as you know, and kept calling, and sending you e-mails that went unanswered just like the phone.

"Then I got the letter from your lawyer, and it nearly cut me off at the knees." Sam's voice choked, but he swallowed hard and pressed on. "It was all pretty clear then. You'd won all that money and didn't want to share it with me. You didn't need me anymore." He looked off into the distance, trying to collect his thoughts.

Ruby touched him lightly on the arm, as if telling him to look at her. "Sam, that wasn't the reason I filed for divorce," she whispered. "That wasn't why. When I learned that you'd been out on that mission after you'd promised me you'd stop, I just couldn't take it anymore. I couldn't spend another day worrying about you. I couldn't bear another moment of wondering whether you'd come back to me, and if you did, whether you'd be in one piece." She glanced down at the mass of scar tissue on his leg and choked back a sob. "I didn't know the full story then. If I had known, I might have understood."

"I know that now, darlin'," Sam said. "I just wish you had told me how you felt a long time ago."

"This is my fault, isn't it?" Ruby asked, her emerald eyes cloudy and filling with tears. "I made this happen. I caused you to be hurt." Her intent might have been to stop her own pain, but she had caused Sam to hurt. How was she going to deal with that? "I was just so tired of putting on a brave front while you went off into harm's way. I couldn't deal with it anymore."

"And you thought that I'd gone on that mission thinking what the little wife at home didn't know wouldn't hurt her, and she'd be none the wiser," Sam concluded.

"Yes, I'd never called you before. I'd always

waited for you to call when you could. I thought that maybe you'd lied about staying behind the lines and had been going off on dangerous missions all along,'' Ruby said, the pain at that realization clearly evident in her clouded green eyes.

"If I'd had the time to as much as e-mail you, Ruby, I would have, but time was of the essence. And I couldn't have told you much, anyway. You know that the nature of my job was classified.''

"I know. And I always hated that part of it.'' Ruby sighed. "But you seemed to love it so much, I didn't want to tell you that. I tried so hard to be a good combat controller's wife, Sam. But I'd just reached the end of my rope.''

Sam sat slowly down on the edge of the tub. "I wish we'd talked like this…before…''

"Me, too,'' Ruby said, her eyes swimming with tears. "Maybe none of this would have happened.''

"Oh, Ruby, don't do that. Stuff happens,'' he said honestly, reaching up to wipe away her tears. "After I got the divorce papers, I volunteered for every mission that came my way. I finally got one that would take our unit closer to the real action. We had to pass through a minefield that had supposedly been cleared, but…''

Ruby gasped and sank to her knees on the cold tile floor. "Oh, God, no. You wouldn't have been on that mission if I—'' She couldn't look at Sam, couldn't face him. She covered her face with her hands and wept.

"Sugar? Ruby honey, look at me.'' Sam's voice was soft and gentle, but Ruby couldn't make herself look up at him, into his pain-filled eyes. "It's not your fault I wasn't careful. I have to take the blame for that all by myself.''

She shook her head, unable to speak through her sobs. How could they have let everything get so out of control?

Over the sound of her weeping, she didn't hear him move, but she sensed when he came closer. She felt his hands rest on her shoulders, just a gentle touch, a caress. ''It's all right, Ruby. I'm here, I'm all in one piece, more or less, and I don't blame you,'' he said, his voice thick with emotion.

''B-but I blame me,'' Ruby replied miserably. ''It was my fault that you put yourself in harm's way.''

''Ruby, look at me.'' His voice was cool and firm, but his hands were gentle and warm as he urged her upward.

She scrambled to her feet with his assistance, but she still couldn't face him. ''I c-can't,'' Ruby sobbed.

''Yes, you can,'' Sam said, his right hand sliding up her arm to her shoulder and then to her chin. He tipped her face up.

Ruby caught one glimpse of his deep gray eyes, then squeezed her own eyes shut. She didn't want to see the blame there.

''Oh, hell,'' Sam muttered, and the next thing Ruby knew, she felt his lips on hers. Not a gentle, tender kiss as before, but a demanding one, a searching one. A welcome one.

She responded to his kiss with all the longing and desire she'd penned up for all those months. She brought her arms up around him and caressed the short hairs at the back of his neck. She felt every bit of hunger and longing he possessed, and she shared her own in kind. Ruby closed her eyes, and it was as if Sam had never been away.

Too bad they hadn't been able to share with words as well as they'd always been able to communicate in the bedroom.

The towel slipped off and Sam pressed his obvious desire against Ruby's stomach. He wanted her to know how much he wanted her, needed her.

Ruby jerked herself away, dragging her mouth from Sam's. They couldn't do this, not now. If they did, they'd just end up in bed, and they'd never be able to work their problems out. Ruby stood back from him, her eyes wide now, her hand at her throat as she tried to still her pounding heart and catch her racing breath.

Sam reached for her, but she shrugged him off.

"I'm sorry, Sam. I just can't do this right now. I have too much to process before I can just fall back into bed with you."

"Who said anything about bed?" he challenged.

"You didn't have to, Sam. Remember, we've been married for ten years. It always ends like this. We never finished an argument because we always ended up making love. And sex can't solve our problem, Sam," Ruby said. "We have to deal with this logically. We have to talk it out."

"And we can't do that with me naked and you in my arms," Sam concluded. He bent down to retrieve the towel. "All right. I admit that I'm disappointed you don't want to make love with me, but I'll wait. If you'll just give me my clothes, I'll dress and go back to the apartment."

"I do want to make love with you, Sam," Ruby said. "More than you know. But I have to keep my mind clear so I can deal with this. Otherwise, it'll just get swept into a corner like all our other problems did. We never really talked through our problems when we were together. We just ignored them and fell into bed.'' She shrugged and smiled sadly. ''We didn't solve anything with sex, wonderful as it always was. Do you understand?''

Sam nodded. ''Yeah. I do,'' he answered huskily.

Ruby stooped to pick up his discarded clothing. ''If you give me a minute, I'll find you something to put on for now. Then I'll cook supper.'' Without giving Sam a chance to call her back, she hurried out of the room.

SAM STOOD in Ruby's bedroom and fingered the sweatshirt and pants she'd laid out for him. He remembered the garments well. They were old exercise clothes that he'd worn years ago and Ruby had refused to throw out. She'd told him once that she wore them when he was away on missions, and she would pretend that he was keeping her warm instead of the worn, gray fabric.

Is that why she'd kept them? Did she still pull them out and wear them when she missed him?

He shrugged. Did it matter? She'd already admitted that she still loved him. Had never stopped. Wasn't that enough of a victory for one day?

The well-worn fabric was soft and smooth as he pulled it over his head. The shirt had been washed so many times it was thin in spots, but it did cover him. And the pants would, too. As he pulled the drawstring tight around his middle, he looked around the room that Ruby had made for herself.

The wooden furniture was warm, just like Ruby,

and the bright yellow curtains and the quilted comforter suited her. He could see her in this room, and he could understand why she had chosen not to bring any of their old furniture here. He hadn't been able to sleep well in their old stuff in the apartment because he'd been besieged by memories. Surely that was the same reason she'd left it there over the store. He looked again at the cheerful colors in the room. Maybe someday they'd make new memories in this room, but for now he'd bide his time. He'd given Ruby a lot to think about tonight, as she had him. Maybe it was best that they hadn't made love.

They had time for that. Now that he was out of the air force, they had the rest of their lives.

He just had to convince Ruby of that.

RUBY PUT THE POTATOES on to boil, then placed a couple of ham steaks in a skillet to cook. In all the excitement of the afternoon, she'd forgotten to get anything else started, and this was as quick as anything. With gravy and a can of peas, the meal would be filling. And working on putting together the meal would serve to keep her mind off what she'd just learned.

Her eyes still burned, but she'd finally managed to stop crying, even if she did have to swallow an occasional sob. Maybe Sam could forgive her, but Ruby wasn't sure she could forgive herself. Her hasty actions had sent him out in an emotional tailspin and had surely been the cause of the carelessness that had led to his injury.

Fresh tears filled her eyes, and Ruby shut them quickly to stanch the flow. "No," she told herself sternly. "You are not going to do this anymore. You are going to feed Sam a filling dinner and then send him home. Then you can think about it. Then you can blame yourself all you want.''

''Blame yourself about what?''

Ruby spun around, to see Sam standing in the doorway. She wondered how much of her impromptu lecture he'd heard, but rationalized that it mustn't have been much or he wouldn't have asked. ''Nothing,'' she said airily. ''I was just giving myself a little pep talk.'' She turned back to the ham sizzling in the skillet. ''Supper will be ready soon.''

''No hurry,'' Sam said, making himself at home in the kitchen. He reached into the cabinets above the counter and collected plates and glasses, then set them on the table. Then he went back for flatware.

They worked together in companionable silence, in a scene that seemed so familiar, yet so alien, considering their recent circumstances. Still, Ruby liked the feeling. It was almost like old times.

Finally, Sam broke the mood. ''Ham? How are you going to face Oscar and Petunia?''

''What?'' Ruby turned to look at him.

Sam arched an eyebrow, cocked his head toward the skillet, then grinned.

''Oh. The ham.'' Ruby felt her face go warm, and she didn't know why. ''It isn't as though I'd met the pig that donated these particular hams, Sam,'' she finally said. ''I'm not a vegetarian, you know.'' She shrugged. ''I guess I just get attached to things too quickly. I hate to lose them.''

''Something tells me we're not talking entirely about Petunia and the kids,'' Sam said, playing with the utensils he'd already set on the table.

''No, I suppose I'm not.'' Ruby tested the potatoes,

then switched off the burner below them. "I just have to mash the potatoes and we can eat."

Sam didn't press the issue, and Ruby didn't elaborate. She wasn't really sure what she'd meant, and she didn't want to have to explain. She just quietly mashed the potatoes, then put them on the table.

She wanted to get supper over with. As much as she loved Sam, she needed him to leave. She had so much to think about. So much to deal with.

And she couldn't think clearly—not about them, anyway—with Sam so close.

"Supper was great, as usual, Ruby," Sam said, picking up his plate and carrying it to the sink. "Even if you were being disloyal to Petunia and the kids." He winked and placed the dishes in the sudsy water.

"I wish you'd drop that bit about the pigs. I hate being reminded that my food was once walking around." Ruby cocked her head toward the scraps on her plate. She pushed herself up and carried her plate to the counter. "Sorry there's no dessert," she said as she scraped her plate into the trash.

"Really? You haven't made dessert once since I've been here." Sam wondered if there was a hidden meaning in that message. Did Ruby want him to stay longer?

"I don't feel like I gave you enough to eat. It was just potatoes and ham and peas, and you worked hard all day."

"Providing entertainment for you and Melinda and Oscar. I swear that pig was laughing at me."

Ruby chuckled. "Well, it was funny. And I wouldn't be surprised if Oscar hadn't been toying with you. You know, pigs are supposed to be very intelligent animals.''

''Smart enough to get you to wait on them hand and foot,'' Sam agreed. ''And to keep them away from the butcher.''

''Don't remind me of that.'' Ruby shuddered. ''Are you sure you've had enough to eat?''

''I'm not hungry, Ruby. At least, not for dessert.'' Sam turned back to the sinkful of dishes. He didn't want Ruby to see the yearning in his eyes.

''I know, Sam,'' she said, and he knew she understood. He also understood why she couldn't give him what he wanted.

He understood it, but he didn't have to like it. ''Well, as soon as my pants are dry, I'll go and leave you alone.'' He rinsed a plate under running water. ''You drying?''

''What?'' Ruby looked as though she were a million miles away. ''Oh. The dishes. Sure, I'll dry.'' She took a towel out of a drawer and reached for the plate he'd just rinsed.

The clothes dryer was still going when they'd finished the dishes. That was fine with Sam. It would give him a little more time with Ruby. ''Well, all done,'' he said, when she had put the last dish away. ''What should we do now?'' He braced both hands on the counter, trapping Ruby between them. Maybe it would work.

Ruby turned, then stopped, realizing the box he'd placed her in. ''What are you doing, Sam?'' she said, impatiently trying to cover her discomfort. ''I don't have time for this silliness.''

''Silliness? You seemed pretty serious earlier.'' Sam reluctantly pulled back and let Ruby go free.

She brushed past him. "Look, Sam. Your clothes are still not dry, but you're decent enough. Wear the sweats back to the apartment. You can bring them back in the morning. It wouldn't hurt for you to have a change of clothes here, considering...."

She didn't finish, but Sam could see the beginnings of a smile play around her mouth.

"Considering that Petunia and Oscar and the others still live here, and farming is a messy business," he finished. Sam sent up a silent "hoo-ah!" If he had extra clothes here, would a toothbrush be far behind? No, it was too soon, so he'd best quit while he was ahead. "Good idea," he said, nodding his head toward the gray sweats. "I'll wash these tonight and bring them back in the morning."

"No need, Sam. It's just as easy for me to do it with the rest of the wash. I'll see you in the morning."

"Maybe not," Sam said. "I think I'm going to go poke around the pavilion a little while before I come over." He stopped. "Damn. I forgot to ask Melinda about the night it fell while she was here."

"She's not going anywhere. Just call her," Ruby said.

"Maybe I will." Sam collected his wallet and car keys off the bathroom sink, then returned to the kitchen. Ruby was standing by the door, looking like a host eager to get rid of a houseguest who had stayed too long. He brushed past her, but instead of going out, he caught her in his arms and kissed her soundly. Then he let go. "See ya," he said, and hurried out the door.

Sam glanced back over his shoulder long enough to see the half smile on Ruby's lips. Yeah, he'd gotten to her. And he was damned pleased with himself. He was making progress. It might be a little slower than he would have wanted, but progress it was. He'd kissed his wife, and she hadn't pushed him away this time.

"Hoo-ah!" he cheered as he slid into the car. "Hoo-ah!"

IT WASN'T UNTIL SAM HAD driven away and Ruby had settled herself in bed that more questions about his injury surfaced. How could he have been injured so severely and she not have known?

When had it happened?

And why, after that phone call the night she'd learned their numbers had won, had it taken so many months for Sam to finally come home?

Ruby punched her pillows and tried to make herself comfortable in her bed. Funny, she'd never slept with Sam in this bed, but now it seemed empty. Now it seemed as if sleeping alone in a bed meant for two was wrong.

No. Ruby sat upright and shook her head. She was not going to let Sam back into her heart...or her bed...until she had all the answers. Until she knew exactly what he expected from her and what she could expect from him. Until then, she was going to proceed with the divorce as if nothing had happened between them. She was going to continue with her plans for the rest of her life without Sam.

Until he proved that he was going to stay.

Ruby yawned and stretched and again tried to make herself a comfortable nest in her bed. At least Sam had said he'd be late in the morning, so if she did have trouble sleeping—and she had no doubt she would—she wouldn't have to worry about Sam finding out about it.

Or asking questions.

Besides, she still had too many of her own.

SAM DIDN'T REALLY KNOW what he was looking for around the fallen pavilion. He wasn't an engineer and he knew nothing about construction, and he sure was too late for finding prints of any kind.

Still, he felt he needed to look at it to get a feel for what had really happened. When he reached the site, he realized that this was a wasted effort. The debris had already been removed, leaving nothing there but a patch of bare earth and a few scattered scraps of charred wood.

He parked the Corvette by the edge of the road and looked at the spot from the window. A few tattered remnants of yellow crime scene tape littered the ground, but the relentless spring winds had long since taken care of most of the tape. As if a couple of strips of plastic tape would keep anybody out. Sam would bet that every citizen of Jester over the age of three had probably poked around the ruins.

He got out of the car and stepped closer. The wood had been gray and weathered or even rotten, and the structure might easily have collapsed from the weight of the snow. So why would anyone try to burn it? Luke did say he had an engineer's report that confirmed his suspicion about the bolts being tampered with.

Sam squatted and tried to get a feel for the place, looking for some sign that might tell him something, anything. Most of the burnt debris had been removed already, but he hoped he could find some tiny shred of evidence that had not been cleared away. He focused on one section of broken timber and spotted what looked like the remains of a bolt. He ran his finger over the broken edge. It was smooth.

He might not be an engineer, but even Sam could tell that this bolt had not broken by accident. It would have been sharp or rough.

"Not much to see, is there?"

Sam looked up as Luke McNeil approached him, trailed by a young woman he didn't recognize. Sam pushed himself to his feet and shielded his eyes from the morning sun as he waited for Luke to reach him. "Nope. I don't know what I expected to find, but I thought maybe I'd get a feel for something." He shrugged. "Nothing jumped out at me."

"Yeah. That's the same feeling I get every time I look at this. I have proof it was tampered with, I have my suspicions, but I can't pin anything on anyone." Luke must have realized that Sam was looking at the woman with him, because he stopped. "Oh, Sam Cade, have you met Jennifer Faulkner? She's Henry Faulkner's granddaughter."

The woman, tall and slender, with a more polished, elegant look than most of the women in Jester, smiled at him and offered her hand. "So you're the mysterious man who's been nosing around town."

Sam grinned as he closed his hand around her fingers. "I must be losing my touch if you noticed me. I was trying to come in under the radar." Her grip was firm, and she met his gaze with startlingly blue eyes.

"No, you're not losing your touch. Luke told me. I'm too much of a newcomer around here to recognize if anything is amiss. I had only come here recently to settle my grandfather's estate,'' she explained.

"But I talked her into staying," Luke said, with a look on his face that was anything but professional.

Sam wondered if something was going on between the two, but he didn't know either one well enough to ask, and neither volunteered any details. Of course, he could ask Ruby. She'd know.

With the gossip brought in by the customers at the Mercantile, there was nothing that happened in town that Ruby didn't hear about sooner or later. The Jester grapevine was nothing if not efficient. If Ruby hadn't heard it firsthand, co-owner Honor Lassiter would have and passed the news on.

Funny how the Jester grapevine worked. Everyone seemed to know everything. Except about who'd tampered with the bolts on the pavilion and who'd tried to burn it.

"Well, it was nice meeting you, Jennifer," Sam said. He turned to Luke. "I guess I'm not going to find anything out here, and Ruby needs me to help her at the farm while that Nick guy is out of town. What do you know about him?" he asked as an afterthought.

"Not much," Luke said. "Seems like a nice enough fellow. Showed up after Ruby bought the old Tanner farm. He's been helping her with the remodeling. Seems to know his business. Doesn't come into town much, and when he does, he's alone."

That should have satisfied Sam, but somehow it didn't. He couldn't imagine Ruby taking up with a drifter, but if Luke didn't know anything about him, Sam reckoned he'd best keep his eyes on the man. It wouldn't be the first time some two-bit con man eased his way into a lonely woman's affections and cheated her out of all her money. And that insinuation in the newspaper had done nothing to assuage Sam's suspicions.

Of course, he'd seen nothing that would indicate that those were Nick's intentions, yet he could not forget finding Ruby in the man's arms the first day he'd gone out to the farm. Or the way he'd tucked her hair so tenderly behind her ear. As if he had every right to.

But from now on, Sam was bound and determined to keep Ruby from easing her loneliness in anyone's arms but his.

"Well, I guess I'll head on out. Ruby's counting on me," Sam said lamely. "I'll try to do some poking around tonight."

"Good enough, Sam," Luke said. "Like I said, I've got my suspicions, but I don't have anything concrete. Anything you find out could help." He took Jennifer by the waist in a courtly manner and steered her back toward his vehicle, parked behind the Corvette.

"Later," Sam said. "I'll see what I can dig up." *And maybe I just might do some digging around about Nick Folger, too,* he thought.

LATER THAT MORNING, Ruby hummed contentedly to herself as she puttered with the growing trays in the greenhouse. This was to be her first paying crop, and she couldn't wait to deliver her first order to Gwen Tanner, who was looking for something other than iceberg lettuce to serve in the boardinghouse.

"There you are."

She jerked around, pulling up more than one lettuce

sprout as she did. "Sam, I didn't hear the car drive up. You startled me."

Sam kissed her quickly on the lips, then stepped back. "Sorry about that, but you were making such a racket that you wouldn't have heard a train wreck."

"I was not," she answered indignantly. Sam had always teased her about her humming, and it felt wonderful to fall into that familiar routine. "Did you learn anything out at the pavilion?"

"Not about the pavilion," he said, pinching off a sprout and sticking it into his mouth. "Luke McNeil was with a very attractive woman, however. It seemed more than a casual acquaintance," he said, munching on the sprout and reaching for another.

"Stop that," she said, slapping his hand away. "I have a paying customer for these greens, and you're eating up all my profits." Ruby picked up her pile of discards and thrust them toward Sam. "Here. If you're hungry, go rinse these off. I bet that was Jennifer Faulkner. She and Luke were childhood sweethearts, but Jen moved away. They picked back up when she came back to settle her grandfather's estate. Now, they're engaged."

Sam arched an eyebrow. "Seems to be going around. First Shelly from the Brimming Cup, then Melinda Hartman. Is there something in the water?" He stopped. "Who's going to buy these twigs, anyway?"

"Gwen Tanner. She wants to serve them in the boardinghouse. She's trying to get a little more upscale with her menus."

"In Jester? Who's going to eat the stuff?" Sam paused. "Speaking of Gwen, when did she get married? Is she part of the marriage boom, too? I couldn't help noticing that she's obviously pregnant, yet I haven't met her husband.''

Ruby pulled off her gardening gloves and grimaced. "Ooh," she said, shaking her head. "That's a touchy subject. Gwen's not married, and she won't say anything about the father. She's just going to raise the child alone, and fixing up the boardinghouse is part of her plan. Not that she really needs to depend on the income from the boardinghouse, what with her part of the lottery money, but she likes to cook and prepare the meals, and she's been enjoying using her money to decorate the place."

Sam leaned back against the growing trays, resting his hands on the edge. "Yeah, well, the boardinghouse is getting a little too elegant for my taste."

"Well, it's Gwen's place, and she didn't ask you." Ruby wished they could steer this conversation to another topic. She was so envious of Gwen and her pregnancy, husband or no. Ruby had longed to be a mother for so long, but she'd never had the courage to become pregnant. Not with Sam going away on those dangerous secret missions so often. Not when she had been so afraid that she might be left to raise the child alone.

Gwen was so much braver than she was. Had Gwen purposely gotten pregnant now that she knew she'd have the money to take care of a child? Ruby's own biological clock had been silently ticking away for years while she waited and hoped that Sam would finally come home to stay. Now she wondered if maybe it was too late, and she'd never get the chance to be a mother.

Chapter Nine

A day later Sam still couldn't help feeling pleased with himself that Ruby had insisted he leave an extra set of clothes at her place. He grinned widely as he drove through the open countryside toward the farm. Though he'd promised himself that he wouldn't push it, he had the shaving kit he'd always kept stocked and ready for middle-of-the-night alerts stashed in the small trunk of the Corvette. It never hurt to be prepared.

And he was determined that Ruby's place would one day be his place as well. No, theirs.

As Sam pulled up to the toolshed, he was startled to see Ruby, looking so much like a farm boy in her straw hat and overhauls as she strode purposefully across the farmyard, pitchfork in hand. One of the piglets trotted eagerly behind her like a stray puppy. He drew the car to a halt in the shade of the shed and climbed out. "Hey, who's your shadow?" he called.

Ruby grinned. "Oscar and I have bonded," she said, offering the pitchfork to Sam. "I'm glad you're here. I wasn't looking forward to turning the compost heap. Seems that job needs more muscles than I have."

"Thanks a bunch," Sam said dryly, taking the fork as Oscar sniffed around his boots, then retreated to hide behind Ruby. "Shouldn't Oscar be in the pen?" Hell, he'd spent half a day nailing that thing together, and it wouldn't keep the damned piglet in? Sam's ego still smarted from Oscar's little escapade the other day, not to mention his knee since it had given out on him in the mud.

"The piglets are fine outside. As long as we keep the greenhouse doors shut so they don't get in and root around in the planting trays, they won't get in the way," Ruby said, removing her hat to brush a bit of flyaway hair out of her eyes and to poke it back behind her ear.

Sam understood Ruby's need to cover up, with her fair skin that tended to burn more than freckle, but he hated her covering her flaming mass of hair. It had been one of the things that had made him notice her in the first place. The breeze sent another tendril of fire across her face, and it stuck to the corner of her mouth. Sam brushed it away and pushed it behind her ear. "There. All fixed," he said. Of course, if she were bald he'd still love her.

Funny, he'd never told her that. Maybe he should.

An idea suddenly came to him. "Say, I stopped by the Heartbreaker last night to do a little nosing around after I left here."

Ruby raised an eyebrow as she returned the straw hat to her head. "In the sweat clothes? I'm sure you were quite the center of attention."

Sam chuckled as he leaned against the pitchfork. "No, I changed first. Dev seems to have fixed the place up since he got married to Amanda Bradley. There has to be something in the water with this wed-

ding boom going on. It's looking more like a fern bar
than a honky-tonk. They're even serving food now.''
He paused, wondering exactly how to word his request.

"Really? Amanda came into the store to buy the
fabric for tablecloths, but I haven't seen the finished
product. The Heartbreaker has never exactly been one
of my hangouts.''

That was something Sam was glad to hear. Not that
he would have expected Ruby to frequent the place.
He couldn't have asked for a better opening than if
he'd filed a request in triplicate. ''Well, let's go check
it out. Tonight. You won't have to cook supper, and
I can treat you to a steak. Hell, we could even try out
the new dance floor.''

Ruby's face lit up with a hundred-watt smile. ''I'd
love that,'' she said. ''Now that we've got so much
done on the farm, we can afford to quit a little early
now and then. And we are millionaires, after all. We
should have people waiting on us for a change. And
I just got a new dress from the Spiegel catalog that
I'd love to wear.''

Now Sam just had to hold on until tonight, when
he'd get to see the new dress and the beautiful woman
in it. Good thing the job Ruby had just assigned him
didn't require much brain power, because all he could
think about right now was tonight, Ruby's new dress
and getting her out of it.

THE PHONE RANG as Ruby was dressing for her
''date'' with Sam. She started to ignore it and let the
answering machine pick it up while she put the final
touches on her makeup, but then she heard Nick's
voice. Ruby hurried to the phone.

"Did you get it?" she asked eagerly, holding the phone carefully away from her headful of rollers. She listened to Nick's explanation, then grinned widely, even if Nick couldn't see it. "*Yes!* I knew you would." This was definitely good news.

They chatted a few minutes, then Ruby drew their conversation to a close. "Okay. I'll see you later." Still grinning widely, she hung up the phone.

The day hadn't started out badly, but it was certainly shaping up to end really well, she couldn't help thinking. Ruby hurried back to her bedroom to finish getting ready for her date with Sam.

She blotted her lipstick, then caught a glimpse of the dress laid across the bed behind her. Maybe it was a little much for Jester, Montana, but Ruby had seen it in the catalog and she'd just had to have it, even when she'd had no idea when or where she'd get a chance to wear it. Then, almost as if it had been preordained, Sam had shown up at her door. It was almost as if it were in someone's plan.

Ruby couldn't remember the last time she'd dressed up and done her hair and worn nail polish, and maybe it was silly, but she was really looking forward to doing so. Looking forward to feeling pretty, feeling like a woman, feeling wanted.

Sitting at the mirrored vanity table, Ruby concentrated on making her hands look like those of a pampered and wealthy woman. She had to chuckle. She might be wealthy by Jester's standards, but considering the last few months, she'd been anything but pampered, and it took longer than she expected.

Ruby had just put on the final coat of polish when she heard the sound of a car on the drive through the open window. She glanced at the clock. How had it gotten so late?

Still wearing the turquoise silk kimono that Sam had brought back from one of his secret trips abroad, Ruby hurried to greet him.

WITH THE EXCEPTION of the first day he'd come to the farm, Sam always used the kitchen door. But today was different. He had a hot date tonight with his wife, and he was going to do everything he could to make it special. He parked the car on the circular drive in front of the house and, donning his new Stetson hat, hurried to the front door.

He felt a little self-conscious in his new outfit, but something told him that the casual civilian clothes he'd been accustomed to wearing during his off-duty hours would not do here. So he'd bitten the bullet, stopped by the Mercantile on the way home and let Honor Lassiter fix him up. He'd sworn her to secrecy so that Ruby would be surprised.

Now he just hoped she wouldn't laugh.

He stepped up on the porch and rapped on the doorjamb. The front door was open with the screen door in place, so Sam could see Ruby coming, and he liked what he saw.

She was wearing the short silk kimono he'd given her years ago, and she held her hands up in the air like a surgeon waiting to put on gloves. The slippery fabric slipped off one shoulder, and Sam had a clear view of her creamy white skin. When she saw him, she stopped.

"Oh, come on, Ruby honey. It ain't that bad," he finally said when she came no closer.

Ruby shook her head slowly. "No, it isn't bad at

all.'' She gestured for him to come in, and Sam, removing his hat, stepped inside. ''When did you get this? Turn around, let me see.'' She gestured in a twirling motion.

Feeling like two kinds of a fool, Sam did as he was told. Hell, even during a stiff military inspection a guy didn't have to pirouette. But dammit, he would do anything if it meant getting Ruby back.

''You look fantastic,'' she finally said, still holding her hands ups.

Sam let out a sigh or relief. ''You like?''

''Oh, yes,'' Ruby enthused. ''I love it. Haven't I been telling you for years that you'd look great in Western wear?''

''Yeah, you have. I got Honor to help me pick it out.'' He looked down at the Western-style shirt and silver belt buckle. ''I feel like I'm in a Halloween costume,'' he said, smiling sheepishly. ''I'd be a whole lot more comfortable in my uniform.''

Ruby smiled. ''Think about it as a cowboy uniform.''

''Yeah. Right.'' Sam nodded toward her odd position. ''What's with the hands? Somebody holding a gun on you?''

''What?'' Ruby slowly lowered her hands to her sides, keeping them away from her body. ''Oh, this. I did my nails, and they weren't quite dry when you got here.'' She held them out in front of her, then waved them around a little bit. ''I guess they're dry by now. I have to finish getting dressed.'' She turned and hurried back toward her bedroom, giving Sam a great view of her long, slender legs as she retreated.

He'd always liked her in that kimono, but then he'd always loved her out of it, too.

Sam stood in the center of the living room and wondered what to do. He fingered the brim of his new hat for a few moments, then took a seat on the couch.

If prior experience had taught him anything, it could be a long wait. And if history were to repeat itself, he knew darn well that the results would be well worth it.

"One more minute and I'll be ready," Ruby called from behind her closed door.

Sam wondered if he should time her, but before he had a chance to check his watch, the door opened. Was she as eager to start their date as he was?

He looked up quickly and stumbled to his feet. "Wow. You sure don't look like a farm girl now," he said as he absorbed the full impact of the stunning, flame-red, sleeveless dress. The brilliant fabric, covering her with all modesty from neck to knee, hugged Ruby's form like a glove, and it was plain to see that working so hard on the farm had done nothing to hurt her slender figure.

She walked toward him on matching high heels that made her long legs seem endless. Sam forced himself to breathe. "You take my breath away, lady in red," he told her, and the words of a song came into his mind. "You're amazing."

"Thank you," Ruby murmured, blushing.

It pleased Sam to know that he could still have that effect on her. Still, if they didn't get going they'd never make it to the Heartbreaker.

Not that it would be a problem for him, but he was going to do it right. For Ruby.

He crooked his arm. "Shall we go?" he said, trying to keep from grinning like an idiot.

Smiling, Ruby looped her arm through his. "Yes,

let's. I can't wait to show off my handsome date in town.''

Sam felt a tightening in his groin, but he willed himself to behave. They'd have all evening, and maybe if the sun and the moon and the planets all lined up just right, tonight would be the night. ''No one will be looking at me,'' he said huskily. Then he escorted her out the door.

Only when he moved his hand to the small of her back as he reached to open the car door for her did he realize that there was no back to the dress. A shiver of excitement surged through him.

Hoo-ah!

Oh man, it was gonna be a long night, he told himself. But he was going to do it right. For Ruby.

It might almost kill him, but he was going to follow her lead.

Thank God Nick was nowhere in sight.

WITH THE EXCEPTION of fresh paint and a new sign, from the outside, the Heartbreaker Saloon looked as it always had. Ruby drew in a deep breath as Sam parked the Corvette in front. The place, if you'd believed Amanda Bradley's complaints before she and Dev Devlin, the owner, had come together, could be loud and rowdy, but for now it looked like any Western-style bar and grill in any city in the country. Would the inside be as comfortable as the exterior seemed to be?

Sam opened the car door and offered his hand to help Ruby out. She accepted. With this low car and these high heels, there was no other way she would have been able to exit the vehicle gracefully. ''Thank you," she murmured, still feeling odd about dating her estranged husband.

Estranged, she thought. Such an odd turn of phrase. There were moments when they did, indeed, feel estranged, but most of the time recently they felt as right together as they always had. It was the other times that made Ruby cautious.

Even if just the scent of his aftershave had her warm and hungry with a hunger that had nothing to do with food.

The sun was still high and the sky bright outside when Sam escorted her through the bat-wing doors into the dark saloon. Ruby, almost blind from the drastic change in lighting, paused just inside. After a moment, her eyes adjusted. The bar's interior looked much the same, too.

No, it didn't, she decided on second thought. Though the same old wooden bar with stools commanded one side, the risqué paintings that had hung above it forever had been draped with sheer fabric. The nude figures were still visible, but only if you made a point of looking. And the mirror above the bar had been polished till it sparkled, a far cry from its dingy, smoke-stained former appearance.

The chairs that flanked the round tables were new, a great improvement over the mismatched ones that had been there before. The most noticeable difference was the addition of rust-and-beige-checkered tablecloths covered with glass, which now gave the bar a more homey feel.

Dev greeted them from behind the bar. "Welcome," he said, as he put down the cloth he'd been using to polish the countertop. "Ruby Cade, you are just the ticket to brighten up the place.'' He turned to Sam. ''You are one lucky man.''

''Yes, I am,'' Sam agreed.

Ruby blushed, but smiled at the compliment as Dev and Sam shook hands. ''Thank you, Dev, but you don't need me. The place looks wonderful.''

Roy Gibson, the bartender, who was a dead ringer for Willie Nelson, came out of the rear, his smile almost broad enough to make a grin. ''Dang interfering woman,'' he grumbled in his Texas accent, still recognizable though he'd been so long in Montana. ''A woman's touch.'' He almost seemed to shudder, but Ruby could see that he was kidding. ''Next thing you know we're gonna have doilies all over the place.''

Sherry Bishop approached them. She'd obviously been hired on to wait tables, and with Sherry having a son bound for college, Ruby was happy she'd been able to find work. Jester had been barely holding its head above water for so long it was wonderful to see the new miniboom in the town's economics.

''Let me show you to a table,'' Sherry said, gesturing toward the dining area. ''Our menu's still a little limited, but we're working on it.''

''I'm sure it will be wonderful, Sherry. I love anything that I don't have to cook.'' With Sam's hand positioned proprietarily at her waist, Ruby followed her to a table.

Sam pulled out a chair and Ruby sat, feeling almost bereft at the loss of his warm hand on her back. Then he seated himself across from her. ''Menus?'' he asked the waitress.

''As I said, it's still a work in progress.'' Sherry clasped her hands in front of her. ''Right now, I can offer burgers and steaks, fries or baked potatoes, and salad with your choice of dressing. And Gwen has baked us some really nice pies. Roy can fix you up anything you want from the bar.'' She smiled. ''So, what can I get you?''

''Steak, rare, and fries for me,'' Sam said. ''Ruby?''

''Salad and a small steak, medium, if you have one,'' Ruby said, looking around. ''I am amazed at what a difference Amanda's few changes have made.''

''She's trying,'' Sherry said.

Sam ordered a beer, and Ruby asked for a margarita. When Sam arched an eyebrow, she laughed. ''I'm not driving. I might have two.''

''Works for me,'' Sam said. He knew what happened to Ruby when she'd had more than one drink. And he'd always enjoyed the results. He wondered if Ruby was trying to tell him something.

Dev delivered their drinks to the table. ''We'll have a band here tomorrow night, but the jukebox works now,'' he said, nodding toward the small stage and an even smaller dance floor. ''Amanda's put some new selections on it. Some nice dance tunes. Feel free.''

Sam took a sip of his beer. ''How 'bout it, Ruby? Want some music?''

''That would be nice. You pick. You know what I like.'' She lifted the large bowl-shaped glass to her lips and tasted the salt on the rim.

''I'll be right back,'' he said, scooting out of his chair.

If Sam remembered correctly, the old selections on the jukebox had run heavily into Hank Williams, Jr.

tunes, and the usual country-western stuff. Now he recognized some popular titles, including "Lady in Red." He couldn't resist. He inserted several coins and then made his selections. Maybe Ruby wouldn't get the symbolism, but a guy could hope.

The strains of his first choice began to fill the air as he sauntered back to her.

Sherry had already served Ruby's salad, and the two of them were discussing the possibility of Ruby providing some of her greens for the restaurant.

"We don't have much ready to sell yet. It's taken me longer to get started than I thought, but I hope to have a crop of leaf lettuce ready in a few weeks. I'll bring in a sample when it's ready to pick," Ruby said.

Sam liked the way Ruby said "we." Did that mean she really was thinking about them as a couple again? He took his seat, reached across the table and squeezed her hand in his.

Ruby looked up and smiled. "What was that for?"

"Why not?" he said, watching Sherry walk away. "I like touching you. Does it bother you?"

"No, it just surprised me. You never used to be very good at public shows of affection." She didn't say she liked it, but she didn't remove her hand, either.

"Do you think Dev and Amanda will use some of our produce?"

"Don't know," Ruby said. "People around here sure are attached to iceberg lettuce."

"Maybe it's just because they've never had the opportunity to try anything else," Sam said, and was rewarded with a nice smile from Ruby. "If you're gonna make a go of your venture, it couldn't hurt to ask around.

"Speaking of business propositions..." he added. "Guess who tracked me down the other day?"

Ruby looked up from her salad. "I have no idea. Who?"

"Cap Horton." Major Capshaw Horton was probably Sam's best friend. He hadn't seen him since Cap had retired several years before, and it was great that he'd looked him up. Cap had always talked about putting his military skills into action when he'd retired. Sam had always gone along with him, but he'd never really believed Cap would carry anything out. Cap had always been more of a schemer and dreamer. Sam had never really expected him to bring his dreams to fruition.

"Is he still going on about you two going into the mercenary business?" Ruby speared a cherry tomato, popped it into her mouth and chewed. She swallowed and made a face. "Hmm, not much flavor. Maybe next year I'll start some tomatoes in the greenhouse."

"Yeah, everybody loves good vine-ripe tomatoes. Why didn't you start any this year?"

"The greenhouses weren't ready. We had a late snowstorm that put us behind schedule."

Realizing that the "us" in Ruby's statement referred to Nick, Sam frowned. He still didn't know what was going on between Nick and Ruby, but he didn't want to ask. For the time being, the man was out of sight. Might as well try to put him out of mind. Sam was damned sure tired of tiptoeing around his wife. He just wanted to get on with the program. Even if his game plan hadn't seemed to be working out the way he'd wanted so far.

"Cap wants to start a real business this time," he said, trying to steer the conversation away from Nick.

"He hadn't worked out the details yet, but he wanted to know if I was in."

Ruby's eyes grew wide with apparent alarm. "You told him no, didn't you?"

Sherry returned with their steaks, sizzling on metal plates, and set them down on the table, interrupting their conversation. "I have steak sauce and ketchup, if you want it. Be back in a jiff with your fries." She turned and scurried toward the kitchen.

"No, I figured I'd wait and see what he's got cooked up. I ain't going into anything that isn't a sound business proposition."

Sam didn't know what Ruby had to worry about, but she looked relieved. She poked at her steak. "If this is a small one, I'd hate to see a big one."

Sam looked down at his own huge steak. "I think *this* is a big one." Of course, Montana was cattle country, so maybe everybody ate steaks this big.

"No, we have bigger," Sherry said, setting a mountainous pile of fries down in front of Sam. "Do you want some ketchup?"

"Yeah, for the fries. How big? And who would eat it?"

Sherry grinned. "You'd be surprised at how many of our good citizens like the big ones. Why, Mayor Larson orders a big one when he comes in."

Sam didn't know the mayor, and he wondered if the mayor would be coming in. Something about the mayor's hotel plan nagged at him. Did Bobby Larson have anything to with the two incidents at the demolished pavilion?

"Eat up," Sherry urged. "I'll be right back with your ketchup."

"We will definitely have to try out the dance

floor,'' Ruby said, causing Sam to utter a silent ''hoo-ah!'' ''Especially if I eat all this steak.''

''You don't have to eat it all, but I'll hold you to that dance.'' Sam cut off a portion of his own steak and lifted it to his mouth. ''Damn, it smells good.''

''Tastes good, too,'' Ruby said, her mouth full. ''Eat, so we can dance.''

''Thought you'd never ask,'' Sam said, then put the piece of meat into his mouth and chewed. Ruby might want him to hurry up and eat so they could dance, but this steak was just too good to rush through. He took a swig of beer.

What more could a guy ask for than a beautiful woman sitting across from him, a good steak and a jukebox to dance to so he could have an excuse to put his arms around her and pull her close?

Someone came in, and Sam glanced up at the bar and almost choked on his steak. Whatever good feelings he might have had crashed and burned as he watched Nick Folger take a seat on one of the high stools and set his hat on the bar. Damn, what the hell was he doing here? Sam glared at his nemesis, and if looks could kill, Nick would be dead on the barroom floor.

Roy set a long-neck beer bottle in front of Nick, and Nick picked it up. He crooked a finger around the neck, lifted it to his mouth and took a long pull on the bottle. Then apparently seeing Sam's glare in the mirror, he lowered the bottle, raised it in a silent toast and took another drink.

Sam didn't know what to make of the gesture, but since Nick seemed content to sit at the bar, and he hadn't approached Ruby, he would leave well enough alone.

He was here with Ruby, and they were going to have a good time. The hell with hippie-cowboy handyman.

RUBY PUT HER FORK DOWN, blotted her lips and uttered a contented sigh. "I did not think that I'd be able to eat all this, but it was so good," she murmured. "I am definitely going to need that dance you promised me to burn it off, though."

"Sure," Sam grunted, his mouth full. He still had a huge amount of steak remaining, and he hadn't even made a dent in his fries.

Ruby reached across the table and picked up a French fry, dipped it in a puddle of ketchup and popped it into her mouth. "Hurry up. You have to save me from these fries," she said, her mouth full. She reached for another, then caught a familiar silhouette from the corner of her eye. "Look, Nick's here. When did he come in?"

"About the time Sherry served our steaks," Sam replied, with a definite note of pique in his voice.

"And you didn't say anything?"

"I figured if he wanted to talk to us, he would," Sam said, cutting off another piece of meat.

Ruby shrugged. "I guess so. I already talked to him on the phone earlier today. His trip to Rapid City was a success."

"Glad to hear it," Sam said, not sounding the least bit like he meant it. "I'm done. Let's dance." He put his napkin on the table and pushed back his chair.

Though surprised by Sam's abruptness, Ruby accepted his invitation. She had enjoyed this evening out, and she looked forward to dancing with her husband, though his comment about Capshaw Horton's proposition had given her a moment's pause. Then she'd remembered about how Cap was always coming up with grand ideas that he never followed through with. This was probably just another one of those.

In the meantime, Ruby would accept any excuse to feel her husband's arms around her.

SAM SELECTED "Lady in Red" again and fed the jukebox more coins, then drew Ruby into his arms. "This one's for you," he said as the music began.

Ruby's mouth widened into a brilliant smile as she recognized the song. "Why, Sam Cade, you romantic devil, you." She pressed herself closer to him and rested her head against his shoulder as they swayed to the music. "I love it," she murmured softly.

It would have been the most perfect moment, but just as Sam was ready to whisper something romantic into Ruby's ear, he caught another glimpse of Nick at the bar. The man lifted his beer in another enigmatic salute, and Sam tried to push away an irrational surge of jealousy.

Why was Nick pestering him? Why in the hell couldn't he have just stayed where he'd come from and left Sam and Ruby alone?

Still, he had Ruby in his arms, and Nick didn't, and Sam supposed he'd won. For now.

But, dammit, if Nick even thought about asking Ruby to dance, they were gonna have it out.

Chapter Ten

Ruby leaned back against the seat as Sam drove them through the dark countryside toward home. For the most part, the evening had gone well, she thought. She was a little confused about why Sam had seemed to get so tense after Nick came in, and there was that vague worry about Cap's business proposal. But Sam hadn't acted as if it was a big deal, so maybe it would blow over.

And even if he had hustled them out earlier than she would have liked, their dinner date had been a success. She sighed. "Almost perfect," Ruby murmured dreamily as they reached the turnoff to the farm.

"What's that?" Sam said as he steered the car down the bumpy lane.

"Oh, nothing." Ruby felt herself grow warm. "I didn't realize I had said it out loud. I was just thinking about what a nice evening it was."

"Yeah, it was," Sam said. "I've missed having you in my arms."

Not as much as I have, Ruby thought, but she didn't say it out loud. She still had doubts about Sam, but as the days went by, those doubts had begun to dwindle.

Sam pulled up in front of the house and parked. As Ruby waited for him to come around and help her out, she wondered what the next step should be. As much as she wanted Sam back in her life, was she ready for more? Did she want him in her bed?

Yes, but on what terms? Until she was sure about that, she would not let him in. No matter how much it hurt her to wait.

Sam opened the door and offered his hand, and Ruby accepted. As their fingers met, another surge of electricity rushed from his hand to hers, and her skin tingled with anticipation. She couldn't help thinking that the thrill was much the same as when they'd first gotten to know each other when they were dating. But, she reminded herself, dating Sam had been easy. Being married to him had been difficult.

They paused under the porch light, and Ruby waited for the expected kiss. How strange it seemed to be standing outside her door waiting for her husband to kiss her, as if they were strangers after a first date and just getting to know one another. But they *were* like strangers after so much time, she supposed, which was why she hadn't welcomed Sam with open arms when he'd come back after those long months of silence. One of these days she would have to ask him about that, but right now she wasn't sure she wanted to know.

Not if it meant learning that there might have been another woman.

Why she suddenly thought that, Ruby didn't know, but that notion cemented her resolve to continue to keep Sam at arm's length. Sam had never given her reason to suspect he had a wandering eye, and his long silence probably had more to do with his injury than anything else. Still, she'd take it as slow as she could until she knew for sure.

He pulled her into his arms and tipped her face up to his. Ruby leaned into his embrace and drew in the fragrance of his aftershave mixed with the scent of beer and apple pie and that essence that was uniquely Sam. Instantly her body became pliant and soft and warm and wanting, but she knew it was still too soon.

Too bad her mind wasn't as good at forgiving as her body was.

Their lips met, and Ruby pressed closer, hungry for the weight of Sam's form against hers. She loved the feel of his lips on hers, the taste of him, the smell of him. She loved him. She wrapped her arms around him and played with the hair, grown longer since he'd been working with her, at the back of his neck.

How easy it would be to lead him into her room and to let him make her his again.

"Ruby, honey," Sam rasped, his south Georgia drawl thicker than usual with emotion. "Let me come in tonight. Let me stay."

Panic rushed through her. She wasn't ready for this yet. Ruby had hoped that Sam wouldn't ask. Wouldn't push. Not this soon, anyway. Frustrated, and panting with want and need, she forced herself to push away, out of his embrace. "I-I-I'm sorry, Sam. I can't. I'm just not ready!"

Sam let her go so abruptly that Ruby almost staggered.

"What the hell is the matter with you, Ruby? Have you found someone else? Is it that damned Nick Folger?" Sam backed up until he could go no farther, halted by one of the porch supports. "What the hell is that man to you, anyway? I'm still your husband until the papers are signed. I think I have the right to know!"

Ruby stared at him, too shocked for a moment to speak. Then a smile twitched her lips. She tried to hold it back, but she couldn't. It was just too, too funny. A giggle slipped out, then a deep, throaty chuckle, then an all-out laugh. The complete absurdity of the situation overwhelmed her, and she couldn't help herself. She almost doubled over laughing.

Sam had imagined any number of responses to this question over the past couple of weeks, but Ruby dissolving into fits of laughter had not been one of them. He swallowed his anger and looked at her, more perplexed than angry.

Obviously, he was a mile off on his suspicions, but he still didn't know what the truth was. "Who the hell is Nick Folger? What is he to you?"

Ruby swallowed a giggle and opened her mouth as if she were going to answer, but all she ended up doing was laughing again—so hard that tears filled her eyes. Finally, with tears streaming down her cheeks, she fell into Sam's arms.

"Ni-Nick," Ruby said, swallowing another giggle. "Nick is my cousin. Maybe if we'd had a big family wedding instead of eloping, or you hadn't been running off on all those top-secret missions and playing hero all the time, maybe if you'd been around here more, you might have had an opportunity to meet him before now." She taunted him with a teasing smile.

"Then why doesn't anybody else in Jester know who he is? Why is everybody in town talking about him as if he's some sort of gigolo fortune hunter?"

"Gigolo? Oh, that is too perfect," Ruby said, trying to speak over her giggles. She wiped at her eyes with a knuckle and shook her head.

"Nick isn't from Jester. He grew up in Rapid City, South Dakota," Ruby explained. "Nick was between jobs, and I needed some help here, so it was a perfect deal for both of us."

"You mean you're paying him?"

"I'm getting the family discount, of course. Nick has an opportunity to buy out the owner of the construction company he'd been working for. The owner was retiring, and his daughter wasn't interested in the company, so he wanted Nick, his foreman for the last few years, to take it over. While Nick was waiting for the deal to be negotiated and the bank to decide whether he was worth the money, he came here to help me get repairs done on the house and the greenhouses built.

"I wanted to lend him the money for the down payment, but he wouldn't hear of it." Ruby gazed directly at Sam, and there was no way he could look into those clear green eyes and not believe her. "He called me earlier to tell me that the loan had finally been approved."

"Damn," Sam muttered. "I am such an idiot. I was so damned jealous of the man." He chuckled himself, finally realizing the wry humor of the situation. "And he's your cousin?"

"Yup. My mom's older sister's boy. She married Horse Folger right out of high school and they moved to Rapid City. Been there ever since. Since Daddy died and Mom remarried and moved to Denver, I don't see Aunt Garnet and Nick that much, so this was a great opportunity to catch up."

"And you didn't think it was important enough to tell me about," Sam said.

"We weren't exactly speaking at the time, Sam," Ruby pointed out. "For all those months I had no idea what was going on with you or where you were, and then all of a sudden you appeared, pale and thin, on my doorstep. What did you expect me to do?"

Sam shrugged. "Hell, I don't know. I had a lot of my own baggage to work through. And I damned sure did not want to come crawling back here to beg you to let me back into your life. I didn't want your pity. All I want is your love. I had to come back to you on my own two feet."

"Pity?" Ruby looked as though he had slapped her. "What do you mean, on your own two feet?"

"The docs weren't sure I was going to keep my leg, much less whether I'd be able to get much use out of it again. It was touch and go for a while, but they finally managed to save it. Then it was a long, hard haul in therapy before I could walk on it."

Sam wasn't sure if having Ruby there to go through it with him would have made a difference in his recovery, but he knew that having her to work for had been one hell of a goal. "I didn't want to come back to you a broken man."

"Oh, Sam. You are not broken. And it wouldn't have mattered to me if you were walking or not. I just wanted a husband I could depend on. One I could count on to be there when I needed you."

"Instead of your cousin Nick?" Sam turned away and looked off into the darkness, suddenly realizing how much he had almost lost in taking that mission the night Ruby had called to tell him that they'd won the Big Draw. "I guess I really screwed up, didn't I?"

Ruby touched him on the shoulder, her hand soft and gentle. "I guess we both messed up, Sam, but it's not too late to try again."

He turned around, careful not to read anything into Ruby's statement that she didn't really mean. "What are you telling me?"

"I think we should give it another try." Ruby drew in a deep breath. "Why don't you go home and get a good night's sleep so that in the morning you can bring all your stuff over."

Sam's breath caught.

"Separate bedrooms for the time being," Ruby said carefully, still surprised by her impromptu invitation. She hadn't planned on asking Sam to move in, but maybe it was a good idea to let him see what life on the farm was all about before they made a permanent decision. And she wanted to make sure Sam didn't have his heart set on any wild schemes with his old buddy Cap Horton.

"Hoo-ah!" Sam said, sweeping Ruby into his arms. "I promise you, Ruby, you will not regret it." He kissed her soundly, then let her go. "I'll let you call all the shots. I was the one who screwed up. But I'll do my damnedest not to repeat my mistakes."

Ruby smiled. "That's all I can ask."

Reluctant to leave, but eager to get home so that tomorrow would come all the sooner, Sam stepped off the porch. "You won't regret this, Ruby," he repeated.

"I know, Sam. I know."

He hurried down the walk to his car.

"And Sam?"

He looked up at her over the top of the Corvette as he pulled open the door. "Yeah?"

"I never stopped loving you. I mean it, Sam. Even if I did try."

"Maybe I didn't do everything the way you thought I should, but I did it all for us," Sam said. Then he climbed into the car and turned the key.

All he had to do was make it through one more endless, lonely night.

SURPRISINGLY, Ruby woke up early, refreshed and rested. She'd expected to toss and turn all night after her hasty decision to let Sam move in, but instead, had fallen into a deep, blissful sleep. She didn't think she'd slept so well since she'd moved out to the farm.

Now she sat in the porch swing, her legs curled up underneath her, enjoying her first cup of coffee of the day as she watched the morning come to life. Meadowlarks called in the distance, and at the sound of an approaching car, a family of deer, a doe and two spotted fawns, scurried across the road toward the trees near the creek.

Ruby smiled. She should have known that Sam would be here bright and early. Of course, maybe that was why she was sitting here on the porch.

Waiting.

For Sam to come home.

The car bumped closer, sending up clouds of dust as it approached down the unpaved country road. Reluctant to leave her cozy seat, but eager to greet her husband, Ruby got up and went inside. She'd have a cup of coffee ready for him, and maybe they could sit for just a few minutes alone on the porch and enjoy the quiet before they started their day.

As Ruby stepped outside with his mug of coffee, Sam pulled into the drive and parked behind the SUV, which Nick had returned. She hurried down the porch steps and met Sam halfway.

"You're up early," she said as he strode up the walk. She offered the steaming cup of coffee to him, and he accepted gratefully. "Where's your stuff?"

"That's all I had." He nodded toward the Corvette. "Didn't want to bother having it shipped here till I was sure I was gonna stay." He accepted the mug and took a long swig. "Yeah," he said. "Just what I needed. I didn't even take the time to make instant this morni—" He stopped abruptly, and Ruby wondered if he was afraid to let her know just how eager he was.

Well, she was eager, and she didn't care who knew it—Sam, Nick, everyone in town. "Yes, I think this is the first time I've gotten up this early without the alarm, too. Come." She patted the seat of the swing. "Join me on the porch while we drink our coffee. Nick will be here soon enough, and I'll have to get breakfast ready."

Sam looked toward the silver-colored trailer where he knew Nick slept. "Have you spoken to him…about… Have you talked to him this morning?"

Ruby chuckled into her coffee mug. "Don't worry, Sam. I won't tell him anything about our little…" She paused long enough to take a deep drink, then sighed. "Our little misunderstanding. We'll just let that be our own secret."

Just then the subject of their conversation stepped out of the trailer. The door swung open wide, sending a flash of morning sun their way. Nick yawned and stretched, then looked toward the house. He must have seen them, for he waved.

"Good morning, Nick," Ruby called, returning his wave. "Come join us. Coffee's ready in the kitchen."

She sighed contentedly and leaned against Sam, snuggling closer to him and relishing the strength and the warmth of his body. This was what she'd imagined when she'd first heard that the Tanner farm was for sale and she'd learned of the lottery win and knew she could finally afford to buy it. This was what she'd wanted Sam to come home to. Now it looked as though it was finally happening.

Nick had detoured through the kitchen for coffee then stepped out through the front door and seated himself in the rocking chair across from them. He took a sip of his coffee and seemed to be waiting for one of them to initiate conversation. Of course, Nick had always been silent and slow to talk. Maybe it was the Native American in him.

"Ruby tells me you got some good news yesterday, Nick," Sam said. "Congratulations."

A huge smile spread across Nick's face, transforming his almost stern expression to a grin. "Yeah, man. It was touch and go there for a while. All I had to offer was some know-how from the Seabees and my reputation. The bank wanted collateral." He chuckled. "I offered 'em my truck and my trailer. They weren't impressed."

"Oh. You're the cousin who was in the navy," Sam said. "I didn't make the connection."

Nick grinned again. "What? With this hair you couldn't tell?"

"Well, you got out of the navy a long time ago," Ruby interjected. "I guess I'd better go start cooking breakfast. As much as I'm enjoying sitting out here, we've got work to do.'' She reluctantly pushed herself out of Sam's arms and got up. ''I guess now that you've got the loan, Nick, you'll be leaving soon.''

''I think I can manage to hang out here long enough to get your kitchen finished,'' Nick told her. Then he grinned again. ''They're delivering your appliances tomorrow afternoon. That means we need to take out the old ones today and get everything ready.''

''*Yes!*'' Ruby cheered. ''I cannot wait to get my new, un-avocado stuff.'' She hurried inside and left Sam and Nick alone to get acquainted. For real this time.

SAM STOOD INSIDE the gutted kitchen and wondered how they were ever going to have this place ready for the appliances to be delivered tomorrow. He rolled up his sleeves and considered taking off his shirt, but if he was hot now, it might still be hotter later in the day. Moving the appliances had been easy, as was pulling up the worn linoleum. The hard part was yet to come.

''Time for a break,'' Ruby said, carrying a platter of sandwiches she had made earlier and stored in the refrigerator, which had been moved to the mudroom.

''Didn't think you'd ever ask,'' Sam said, gratefully taking one and looking around for a place to sit.

''I thought we'd go out on the front porch again,'' Ruby said, seeming to read his mind. Of course, she'd always been able to anticipate his needs. Maybe if he'd been as good at figuring out hers, they wouldn't be in this fix now, Sam thought.

Nick came in, shirtless, his dark skin glistening

with sweat. Funny, Sam thought, yesterday he would have been green with jealousy—as green as those appliances they'd taken out. But today it was just Nick, no longer a threat, but a friend.

Sam chuckled and tossed a canned soda at his former rival.

"Something funny, man?" Nick caught the can adeptly and popped the top.

"Naw. Just remembered something." He shrugged. "You had to be there." And Sam was damned glad that Nick hadn't been there in his head when he had been thinking so ill of the man. You learned a lot about a man working side by side with him, whether on a combat control team or a work crew. Of course, he'd been too blind with jealousy to notice until now.

Maybe if he hadn't been so overwhelmed with all that uncertainty about Ruby, he might have figured Nick out sooner.

"Come on, you guys. The more time you waste fooling around, the longer it will be before my beautiful new kitchen is up and running," Ruby called, beckoning them toward the porch.

The sun had moved to the other side of the house, leaving the porch in blissful shade. In Georgia, where Sam had grown up, a little bit of shade wouldn't have made that much difference, but in the low humidity of the high plains it was as different from full sunlight as night from day. Winters in Montana might be brutal, but Sam suspected his attitude was more of the Southern phobia about cold weather than a real dislike. He'd made it through an assignment in Alaska, and the comfortable summers there more than made up for the cold winters. Sam looked out into the beautiful, sunny day. And if this was what summer was like, maybe he wouldn't mind it so much.

Not as long as he had Ruby in his bed to snuggle up to and keep him warm on those cold winter nights.

"You know anything about wiring, Sam?"

Sam looked up, not sure he'd heard the question. "As in electricity?" He shook his head. "Not a heck of a lot. How much wiring we got to do?"

Nick shrugged. "You saw the kitchen. We're gonna need a lot. Good thing I have that electrician coming in from Pine Run tomorrow morning. I can do some, but I want to make sure whatever gets done is up to code."

"Amen to that," Sam said.

"What kind of code?" Ruby looked up from her tuna sandwich.

"Electrical code," Nick clarified. "I don't have an electrician's license here in Montana, and I don't know what all the regulations are. Better safe than sorry."

Ruby frowned. "I guess I can't quarrel with that." She took another bite of her sandwich and chewed thoughtfully. "Are you sure you'll be able to get all that done in one day?"

"Nope. It might take a couple," Nick said.

"Several days?" Ruby wailed with obvious dismay. "What are we going to do for food until then?"

Nick looked at her. "What's the big deal? We've got sandwich stuff. Cereal for breakfast. We'll survive."

"You can put the coffeemaker in the living room and it'll work fine," Sam said. "And I happen to know of a nice little place in Jester where they make great steaks and have a jukebox to dance to."

"Burgers there aren't bad, either," Nick added. "It'll only be for a few days, Ruby. Think about what it'll be like when we're done. Don't dwell on what you're gonna be doing without while you're waiting."

"Yeah, sure. You haven't been working with antique equipment while you've been waiting," Ruby said sourly. "And living without a microwave oven," she added.

Nick glanced over his shoulder toward the rounded shape of his travel trailer, glinting bright in the noonday sun. "Oh, yeah?"

"And you've never had to eat raw rattlesnake when there was nothing else," Sam said, remembering his two weeks of desert survival school with a shudder.

Ruby lifted her hands in a gesture of surrender. "Okay, okay. I give up. I know I've been spoiled with all my modern conveniences, but I am a millionaire, after all. I expect you both to take me out to the Heartbreaker for dinner tomorrow night," she said primly. "I want to be the talk of the town, coming in with two handsome men on a date."

They'd already been the talk of the town, but if Ruby had already forgotten the accounts of their problems in the paper, Sam wasn't about to remind her.

He looked at Ruby, her coppery hair fluttering about her face in the light summer breeze. She was what really mattered to him.

Without Ruby in his life, he had nothing.

RUBY STOOD IN THE DOORWAY and watched as Sam and Nick worked together with the silent precision of a surgeon and his scrub nurse. They seemed to have little to say, and what words were spoken were terse and concise, but it was easy to see that the tension between them had lessened. They even managed to share an occasional laugh, though Ruby didn't know what they thought was so funny.

As long as they were getting along, it didn't matter what they were laughing about.

Ruby had been so excited about the new kitchen equipment being delivered that she had almost missed seeing the friendship forming between Sam and Nick. But once she had noticed, it was good to see. Maybe it was because they both had a military background that they seemed to be able to anticipate each other's needs, or maybe there was some sort of silent communication that went on between men that women would never understand.

Whatever it was, it was better than the silent rivalry and the angry stares.

Standing in the middle of the barren kitchen, Ruby found it difficult to imagine that it would ever be the beautiful, modern kitchen she had imagined. Though Nick assured her that the details were coming together right on schedule, she looked at the empty expanse with a growing sense of dismay. She knew, of course, that Nick had held off making many of the physical changes necessary to the kitchen until now because she'd still needed to use it, but the amount of work remaining to be done seemed daunting to her inexperienced eyes.

Not knowing whether to be discouraged or hopeful, Ruby leaned against an exposed wall stud and let out an impatient puff of breath.

Waiting was one of the things that she had hated so much about being an air force wife. She had thought she knew what to expect when she'd married

Sam, but the reality proved far more taxing than the romantic notion she'd had about it all before she'd actually lived it. She hated waiting and wondering when she wanted to be in the thick of things. Of course, she'd never been able to fly a plane or jump out of one, so rather than finding something else that interested her, she'd stayed home and pouted.

The realization came as a sudden revelation to her. Had she been the one in the wrong?

She'd have to think about that, but not now. Now she was about to go out of her mind.

Her head ached from the constant hammering and the raucous drone of the circular saw, and she rubbed her temples tiredly. She had to get away from the noise and the sawdust. She had to get out of here.

"I'm going to go to town," Ruby announced, not caring whether the men answered her or not. "Honor said we're supposed to be getting a new shipment of fabrics in at the Mercantile today, and I want to pick something out for curtains for the kitchen. Honor said the wallpaper I ordered came in, too."

"Good idea," Nick said. "Pick up some more finishing nails and a few other things for me at Faulkner's Hardware, okay? I'll make a list."

"Anything you need, Sam?" Ruby asked petulantly as Nick got up to make his list. Here she'd expected that she would be the center of attention between her two favorite men now that Sam had stopped competing with Nick, and suddenly they were treating her like some kind of lowly errand boy.

Maybe this newfound friendship wasn't such a good thing, after all.

"Only you, darlin'. Only you," Sam said, his gray eyes glistening, and every one of Ruby's disgruntled feelings simply melted away.

Chapter Eleven

"I saw Sam this morning," Honor Lassiter announced as soon as Ruby entered the Mercantile. "He said he was moving out to the farm. Is the divorce off?" she asked, sotto voce.

Ruby looked around the store to see if anyone was listening. She didn't need any more snippets of her private life showing up in the newspaper. The account of her date at the Heartbreaker had been innocuous enough, but it had still been an invasion of her privacy.

With the exception of two of their own employees, who were busy shelving baby clothes in the children's section, they seemed to be alone. But she wasn't about to take any chances until she knew who was behind the gossip, so she dragged Honor into the office and closed the door just to be on the safe side.

"I don't know if we're getting together or not," Ruby said. And she didn't know. She was still wondering what had made her issue that invitation, especially after Sam's accusation, but having him move out there just seemed like the natural next step.

"Why don't you know?" Honor demanded, flicking her long, honey-blond hair over her shoulder. "He's gorgeous, and he obviously wants you back."

Ruby sank into the swivel chair in front of the roll-top desk. "I know," she said. "But I need to be sure he's lost his need for excitement. I'm afraid life in Jester, Montana, might prove too boring for him after a while. You know, how can you keep him down on the farm after he's seen the world?"

"Stop thinking in the negative, Ruby," Honor said. "He came looking for you. Not a lot of men would do that after what you did to him."

Ruby felt as though she'd been smacked. "What do you mean, after what I did to him? He was the one who broke his promise to me. What was I supposed to do?"

"Did you ever ask him why?" Honor asked simply. "Did you give him a chance to explain?"

"Not until the other day," Ruby said. "I jumped to conclusions, and I should have waited to find out what the circumstances were." She drew in a deep breath. "And it was my fault he got hurt," she said.

"How can that be?" Honor asked, taking a seat on a ladder-back chair across from Ruby. "You were nowhere around him."

"Oh, Honor, I really messed up." Ruby looked over at her friend and struggled to hold back her tears. "Sam and I have talked about how he got his injury." She drew in a long shuddering breath. "He said when he heard that I wanted out of the marriage, he thought I didn't love him anymore, and he started taking chances. He walked into a minefield and almost lost his leg because of me."

Honor blinked her large, gray eyes, but didn't comment on Ruby's confession.

"I've shocked you, haven't I?"

"But you didn't mean to have that happen, Ruby. You didn't know it would happen."

"That's true. And I've tried to explain to him that I didn't want out because I didn't love him anymore, but because I loved him too much."

"Did he understand?"

Ruby drew in a deep breath and clenched her hands in her lap. "He seemed to, but how can I be sure? I have to be positive I won't find myself left at home again and waiting for him to come back from some other dangerous missions. I don't think my battered heart could handle any more hurts."

Honor took a deep breath, reached over and clasped Ruby's hands in hers. "You can, Ruby. You can. You've found yourself a wonderful man who obviously loves you, but you don't seem to believe that you deserve to be happy."

Swiping at a tear, Ruby swallowed. "Maybe you're right. I was so unfair to Sam, and I jumped to so many wrong conclusions. I know that now, but what do I do about it? How do I make it right with Sam?"

"You're asking me? I'm hardly the one to ask about relationships. I've pretty much given up on finding love myself, even if I am stupid enough to keep hoping."

"Oh, Honor. We are a couple of sad characters, aren't we?" Ruby let go of Honor's hand, reached behind her and snapped a tissue out of the box she kept on the desk. "I have a husband I'm not sure I can keep, and you'd give anything for half of what I have, and can't seem to find it." She blotted her eyes. "Do I look all right?"

"You always look gorgeous, Ruby," Honor said. "Now let's go check out that new curtain fabric."

Ruby nodded and blotted her face with a fresh tissue. "Okay, let's go." She opened the door, then stopped before going into the main store. "You know, Hon, maybe you're looking in the wrong place."

"You may be right. What do you think about me taking a trip to some big city, like New York or San Francisco?"

"I think it's a terrific idea. It's not like you can't afford it," Ruby said, stepping out into the store. She bumped right into Wyla Thorne, local busybody and sourpuss since the lottery win.

"Humph," Wyla grumbled. "You just have to rub it in, don't you?" the woman said bitterly. It was no secret that Wyla had been disgruntled because she'd not contributed to the lottery pool the week they'd won. She'd gone all over town complaining that Jack Hartman, who put in a dollar that week instead of her, had stolen her fortune, though in fact the decision not to play the lottery that time had been hers alone.

Ruby would have thought Wyla was over it by now, but she was obviously still suffering from a major case of sour grapes. "Good afternoon, Wyla," she said as pleasantly as she could. "What can I help you with today?"

"I heard you had some new summer clothes in, and I thought my wardrobe could stand some upgrading," Wyla said, apparently happy to be the center of attention.

Honor arched an eyebrow, which, fortunately, Wyla couldn't see, as Ruby steered the woman toward the ladies' section. Wyla Thorne had a penchant for tight polyester and Capri pants in garish colors that usually clashed with her flaming, obviously-from-a-bottle red hair, and Ruby was certain that she and Honor had not ordered anything like that. She didn't know where Wyla got her clothing, but it hadn't been at the Mercantile since Ruby had become co-owner.

"This is the latest shipment in, Wyla," Ruby told her. "Surely there's something here that will suit your fancy."

As Wyla began shuffling through the rack, Ruby drew in a deep breath.

One could only hope!

SAM CAME BACK around the corner and hung the phone back on its cradle on the wall. "That was Sheriff McNeil. He wants me to come into town tomorrow morning to help him with something." Sam didn't know how much he should mention to Nick about his amateur sleuthing, but figured he'd divulge details on a need-to-know basis only. "Are you going to need my help with anything?"

Nick looked up from where he was making marks on the stripped-down walls. "Nope. I figure me and the electrician will have our hands full."

He didn't say, "Without you in the way," but Sam suspected that's what he meant.

"Great. I'll go out in the morning and be back by noon. Later, if necessary. You reckon you'll be done with the wiring by then?"

"Ought to be."

"All right then." Sometimes Nick could be a little too silent, as far as Sam was concerned. He glanced at his watch. "Damn, it's after six. Where the hell is Ruby?"

"I figure she'll be here when she's ready," Nick said philosophically.

Well, Sam was ready for her now. He'd thought that moving out to the farm would bring them closer, but he was here and now Ruby was in town, while last week the opposite had been true. "What could be taking so long?"

"I'm glad to know you care, Sam," Ruby said from the dining room doorway. She was holding a couple of brown paper sacks that were filling the air with a mouthwatering aroma.

Sam's stomach clenched. "Tell me that's food you have there and you will be forgiven."

Ruby waltzed over and pecked Sam on the cheek. "Gosh, I thought I was going to be a hero just for bringing dinner. What did I do to be forgiven for?"

"Kept me waiting, woman," Sam growled, reaching for one of the bags.

Ruby jerked it away. "No, you don't. You and Nick go get washed up while I put this on the table."

"Yes, Mother," Nick said, straightening. He turned to Sam. "I'll take the bathroom in the trailer. You can clean up in here."

Sam saluted. "Aye-aye, sir!"

"WYLA THORNE CAME INTO the store while I was there," Ruby commented as they sat around the formal dining room table and ate their take-out burgers.

"There's something unusual about that?" Sam asked, his mouth full.

Ruby shrugged. "No. But she's still suffering from a major case of sour grapes, and she didn't make a secret about it." And she didn't find anything in the store that "suited" her, either, Ruby thought sourly.

Even if she had taken up at least an hour of Honor's time.

"Sour grapes about what?" Nick put down an empty piece of waxed paper and reached into the brown paper bag for another burger.

Ruby chuckled. "I'm glad I thought to get two for each of you. I should have known you'd be starving." She popped a French fry into her mouth and chewed thoughtfully. "Wyla is mad because she didn't put any money in the lottery kitty that week. Said she was tired of throwing good money after bad. And, of course, that was the very week they drew our numbers."

"And now she's mad at everyone but herself because she didn't follow through," Sam concluded.

"Exactly. Dean Kenning made a special trip all the way out to her farm and double-checked to make sure she didn't want to enter that week before he drove over to Pine Run to buy the tickets. Wyla said no."

"Then she doesn't have a leg to stand on," Nick said, eyeing Ruby's uneaten fries.

Ruby shoved the cardboard carton of fries in Nick's direction. "Here, go ahead. I don't want them." She dusted the salt off her hands and wiped them on a paper napkin. "I know that, you know that, even Wyla knows that she has no claim on the money. She's just really, really put out with herself that she didn't put her dollar in that week."

"And she's taking it out on everybody else," both men concluded at the same time.

"That's it in a nutshell," Ruby said. "And it wasn't as though she was easy to get along with in the first place."

Nick polished off the last bite of his burger and

shoved a fry into his mouth. "I'm off. You two don't need me here."

Ruby started to protest, but decided she was glad that he was leaving her alone with Sam. They had a lot to work through. Although Ruby wasn't sure how much of their reconciliation would really be work.

She'd never stopped loving Sam, even if she had tried her best. Now she just had to figure out how to let Sam think he'd won her back without seeming too eager.

She was pretty sure her stubborn pride had made her jump to conclusions without hearing Sam's side of the story, and now that she knew more about what had really happened, she regretted her hasty decision. She was certainly embarrassed that their marital problems had become the talk of the town.

SAM ARRIVED at the city dump at the appointed time, but no one else was there. What business they had there, he didn't know, but maybe the sheriff just wanted to be sure that there was no one around to listen to them talk. It wasn't exactly the garden spot of Jester, Montana, and even the early morning breeze couldn't disguise the stench of the garbage.

Luke was a few minutes late, and Sam waited impatiently, rubbing his early morning stubble and drumming his fingers against the steering wheel of the SUV he'd borrowed from Ruby. He had to admit that the big vehicle handled a lot better than the sports car did on these rutted country roads.

It was still far from certain if Ruby would let him stay. After all, she'd left him to sleep all alone in the spare bedroom last night. What would it take to convince her that he was finally home for good?

Sam looked up as he heard the sound of an approaching vehicle and recognized the dark-colored sport utility with Sheriff's Department markings that Luke McNeil drove when on duty. Sam stepped out of Ruby's SUV and waited while Luke drew to a halt beside him.

"What's up?" Sam said as soon as Luke got out of the car. "Haven't you already gone through all the garbage out here?"

"Yeah, I have," Luke said, shrugging. "I just wanted to be sure no one was listening."

Sam looked around at the bleak landscape and the malodorous mounds of trash. The only signs of life were the birds pecking around in the debris. "Can't see that we'd be overheard here," he said. "What have you dug up?"

"Not a hell of a lot past the engineer's report on the pavilion collapse," Luke said. "My face is too well known around here. I don't have the anonymity to listen at doors that I need."

"And you think I do?" Sam commented archly.

"More so than me," Luke said. "And I sure would like to find out who's been feeding all the gossip about everyone in Jester to the *Pine Run Plain Talker* and their 'Neighborly Nuggets' column."

"I'm thinking it might be that Thorne woman. Ruby commented yesterday that she's been grumbling about being cheated out of her part of the money," Sam said. "I don't know the woman, but from what Ruby said about her, it sounds like just the kind of thing her type would do."

"I wouldn't be surprised, either," Luke agreed, looking around as if he expected Wyla to be lurking behind a pile of trash. "But I have no proof. Hell, I talked to the gossip columnist in Pine Run. She said she has no idea who's been calling her. Just that it's the same woman all the time. Apparently, the reporter's come to recognize the caller's voice.''

Sam leaned back against the red SUV and drew in a deep breath. ''I don't suppose the paper has caller ID?''

''Yeah, they have it. It's one of the first questions I asked. All of the calls have come from pay phones in Jester.''

''That narrows things down some,'' Sam said, not trying to disguise his sarcasm. ''We have a woman who has access to pay phones in Jester.'' He laughed dryly. ''It does eliminate about half the population.''

''More than that,'' Luke said. ''There are the targets of her little news flashes. That eliminates most of the millionaires. I don't think it's a coincidence that most of the stories have dealt with them.''

''Well,'' Sam said, ''I've got the morning off, since Nick is working on the wiring. I'll just do some skulking around in town and see what I can hear. The good news is that I don't know that many people around here.''

''And our chief suspect doesn't know you.''

''I'll try to keep it that way, Sheriff. Anything else you need to tell me?''

Luke shook his head. ''Nope. You won't have any trouble spotting Wyla Thorne. She looks like she buys all her clothing at a cut-rate polyester outlet. And her hair is a phony shade of red that never appeared in nature. You can't miss her.''

''What do you want me to do if I find anything?''

''Just come back to me. I'm still trying to figure

out how to handle that one. It isn't slander if the news is true.''

"You just don't want her to get away with it," Sam concluded.

"No," Luke said emphatically. "And I want her to stop." He climbed back up into his official sheriff's department vehicle and started the engine. He chuckled over the roar of the engine. "Of course, it would make my day if we could figure out some way to put the fear of prosecution into her."

SAM LET HIMSELF into the empty apartment over the Mercantile. He had left some dirty clothes there when he'd hastily moved his things out to the farm, and now he was happy that he had. He figured they'd be just what he needed to become less noticeable as he made his rounds through town.

He hadn't shaved this morning, and he'd started to let his hair grow out of the short military cut he'd worn for so many years. That would certainly help in his undercover assignment.

He pulled the shirt and crumpled jeans out of the hamper and wrinkled his nose at the sour odor coming from them. He made a face. If he wore these, no one would get close enough to get a good look at him.

Shaking them with the hopes of dislodging some of the dust and odor, Sam wondered what else he might use to further his disguise. It had been easy enough to skulk around in the shadows a few weeks ago when he'd come into town, because no one had been expecting him.

Now, though he was still a stranger to a good many of the townspeople, he was known, especially since his "date" with his wife a few nights ago had been the subject of the gossip column in the *Pine Run Plain Talker*. He hoped, though, that people would be thinking about the lucky man with the good-looking woman in the red dress and not about the shabby bum he was going to try to become.

Sam laid his clean clothes carefully on the bed and put on the dirty ones. He would definitely have to shower before he went back to the farm. He wasn't sure he would be able to stand himself in this getup for long, much less show himself to Ruby.

He chuckled as he glanced at himself in the mirror. "One look at me and Ruby would be sure to send me packing." And Sam was not about to let that happen.

He rummaged around in the storage closet he'd yet to clean out and found a scuffed and dusty pair of combat boots. He'd be more in place in boots of the cowboy variety, but the ones out at the farm were too new. Necessity was the mother of invention, so he was improvising as best he could.

"Yeah. That'll do it," Sam said to himself after one last inspection in the mirror. Not exactly military spit and polish, but that had been the object.

Now all he had to do was get out of the store without anybody noticing him.

Sam slipped out the back door and down the outdoor stairway without being seen. Not that he expected much traffic in the alley behind the store. The only obstacle might have been a delivery truck, and even then delivery people would probably not have paid a moment's attention to him. Still, it was better this way.

There was a fresh oil stain on the parking lot and Sam rubbed his hand in it, then worked the grease under his nails the best he could, smearing some across his stubbly cheek. It would be tough to get it off tonight, Sam thought, but he'd been dirtier than this before and lived. He wiped his hands on his shirt, scuffed his boots in the gravel by the curb and figured he was good to go.

He tucked in the front half of his grubby T-shirt, leaving the tail hanging out, then sauntered out of the alley onto Big Draw Drive.

James Bond, he was certainly not.

Chapter Twelve

Since Sam had gone into Jester to play detective and Nick was busy with the electrician, Ruby had to find something to keep herself out of the way. As excited as she was about seeing the new kitchen come together in front of her very eyes, she knew that hovering would not help the work get done any faster.

She'd spent so much time working to get the house livable and to get the farm sheds ready that she'd neglected the yard around the house. Yes, she'd kept the weeds that passed for grass mowed, but they'd have to put a real lawn in sooner or later. And the flower beds had all but been ignored.

"I guess now is as good a time as any," Ruby said to herself as she gathered up her gardening equipment from the toolshed and hurried around to the front of the house. The sun had moved to the west, so the unkempt flower bed was in the shade.

Ruby drew in a deep breath, set her basket down beside her and took a good look. Just like the yard, there were more weeds than anything, but oddly enough, two brave yellow blossoms seemed to shine out of the brushy mess. Two yellow roses. Funny she'd never noticed them before.

She hadn't even thought to look at this neglected bed of flowers before today. And now that she had, she'd found the roses. Sort of like the cloud with a silver lining, she thought.

She began to pull weeds from around the leggy, thorny shrubs. The bushes seemed healthy in spite of their overgrown condition. With a little tender loving care, she could return them to their former vigor.

Could she possibly do the same thing with her marriage? Could this be a sign that maybe the mess between her and Sam was not as impossible as it had once seemed?

"You were unfair to him, you know," Ruby told herself as she tugged at the weeds. She hadn't even let him give his side of the story until recently. Due process, it was called.

She'd been judge and jury without giving Sam a chance to tell his version of events. Of course, she knew that now, but it seemed as if too much water had gone under the bridge for them to go back to the way things were before.

No, she wasn't going to think of that. She had never really stopped loving Sam. And she would do everything she could to put their marriage back together.

If she could bring this garden back from weeds, surely she could save her marriage. It hadn't been neglected as long.

SAM'S STOMACH GROWLED as he pretended to browse through the selections in Ex-Libris, Amanda Devlin's bookstore. There was a tempting array of cookies and pastries baked by Gwen Tanner from the boarding-house on a table near a coffeepot, but considering his current state of disreputability, he thought it best to stay away from the tray. The store's pretty and uptight proprietor had been watching him like a hawk since he'd come in, not unlike most of the business owners in places he'd visited today.

If he were running the place, he'd probably do the same thing. He glanced at the clock on the wall above the cash register. Nearly four. The store would be closing soon, so he might as well leave.

Hell, he might as well call it a day. With the exception of the Heartbreaker, Jester pretty much rolled up its sidewalks by six, anyway. It appeared as if he wasn't going to learn anything new today. Sam blew out a frustrated sigh and headed for the door.

"Thank you, ma'am," he murmured, touching the grubby ball cap he'd traded a trucker for at Tex's Garage. Sam pushed through the door.

Amanda nodded in acknowledgment, but so slightly it barely caused her light brown hair to move. The bell over the door tinkled a cheerful farewell, but Sam was pretty sure he would not hear an invitation to "come again." Not that he expected one.

He chuckled. Might as well hurry back to the apartment and get cleaned up. After all, he and Ruby had a dinner date, even if Nick would be coming along to chaperon. The good news was that Nick would not be coming back to the house with them.

As long as Sam got some time alone with Ruby, he was certain they would eventually work through whatever reservations were still holding Ruby back. He just didn't know how much longer he could bear to wait.

He passed the Jester Savings and Loan Office and paused at the corner in front of Kenning's Barber

Shop. There wasn't a lick of traffic on Main Street, but old habits died hard, and Sam stopped to look and listen. And it was fortunate that he did.

A woman who had to be Wyla Thorne darted across the street from the Crowning Glory Hair Salon into Cozy's Drug Store. Surely there couldn't be two people in a town as small as Jester who wore such tacky clothes! And her bright red hair looked more like it belonged on a circus clown than a human being.

The clincher was that one of the few pay phones in town was located in Cozy's. It was worth checking out. Sam had enough cash in his pocket to purchase a magazine, and maybe he'd hear something.

He hurried across the street and stepped inside the old-fashioned drugstore. Another one of those bells above the door jangled, and a man in a white jacket greeted him from behind the pharmacist's window. "Hello," the man said. "May I help you with something?"

Sam looked down. "No, thanks," he mumbled. "Just wanna scope out a magazine."

The magazine rack was located conveniently close to the pay phone, but Sam started at the opposite end. Pretending to scan the titles for something of interest, he slowly made his way in the direction of the redhead using the phone.

"…certain single co-owner of Jester's only department store is planning to take her lottery winnings and go on a whirlwind trip." The woman's laugh sounded like the cackle of a witch. "I bet she's off to have a fling with somebody in the big city."

The woman abruptly hung up, glanced furtively

over her shoulder and looked startled to see Sam so close. Then she hurried out.

"If that didn't sound incriminating, I don't know what does," he muttered to himself.

"What say?" the pharmacist asked.

Oops. Sam had forgotten the man was there. "Uh, just talking to myself. You the guy I pay for this?" He held up a copy of a crime magazine.

"Sure," the man said. "I'll be right out to ring you up."

Sam produced the requisite amount of money, passed it over the counter and, without meeting the pharmacist's eye, accepted his change. "Thanks," he murmured, then sauntered out.

He supposed what he'd overheard could be classified as coincidence, and there was no way he could prove who Wyla Thorne had called, but he'd bet Luke could certainly find out. As soon as he was back outside, he rolled the magazine, shoved it in his back pocket and turned into the Mercantile.

He greeted one of the shop workers, then trudged up the inside stairs. He had to get out of those clothes.

But first he had to tell Luke what he'd found out.

Sam closed the door behind him and began peeling out of the filthy clothes as he headed for the phone, an extension of the store number that Ruby had connected. As he dialed, he sat down on the recliner, and when the phone rang, he began to work at the long row of laces up the front of his boots.

He got the dispatcher, who said the sheriff was unavailable, but that she could contact a deputy if he needed him. "Uh, no need. I'll try Luke at home."

But Luke didn't answer at home, either. That was odd. He wondered where Luke had got off to.

Sam shrugged. He'd just have to see if that particular tidbit showed up in the *Plain Talker* anytime soon. And he'd report to Luke when he found him.

Sam hung up the phone, then stripped out of the rest of his clothes and hurried to the shower. The water was cold, but he didn't care. His blood was cooking enough to compensate. Sam didn't know what Wyla Thorne thought she would accomplish by telling tales about the residents of this town, but it was damned sure annoying.

At least he knew that Ruby wasn't going anywhere, so that must mean Honor was. He wondered if Ruby knew what was going on.

Sam stepped out of the shower. The sooner he dressed, the sooner he could ask her. Hell, who cared what Ruby knew about Honor's plans? He just wanted to get home.

To Ruby.

RUBY LOOKED UP from perusing a seed catalog and shopping for ideas on plants to use in the new flower bed, and smiled at the sound of the car door slamming.

"Hey, what's the deal with the flower bed out front? It looks naked," Sam called through the screen door as he hurried up the porch steps.

Ruby loved the way Sam said ''nekkid'' when he meant naked. It was so adorably Southern. Of course, she liked it better when it was uttered in connection with the two of them. It had been far too long since she'd been ''nekkid'' with her husband. She felt her face grow warm, and she fanned herself with the seed catalog just as Sam came inside. He was dressed in jeans and another Western shirt, and he looked absolutely terrific. "Hi," she called brightly, hoping he wouldn't notice her flushed condition. "You were gone a long time."

"Yes, but I think I found out who's been telling the *Plain Talker* about everybody in Jester's business." He sank to the couch beside her. "Shouldn't you be getting ready by now?"

Ruby had completely forgotten about their "date" tonight. After doing without the kitchen for two days, she was ready for a hot meal, especially one that someone else cooked. She tossed the catalog aside and got up. "I am so sorry, Sam. I completely forgot about dinner."

Sam frowned in disappointment look, but Ruby could see he was teasing. "How soon they forget," he drawled. "You really know how to hurt a guy."

She started to lean in to kiss him, but decided not to at the last minute and jerked back. Sam had obviously just showered, and she looked like—and smelled like—she'd been working in the yard all afternoon.

"I'll just be a couple of minutes. I only meant to look through the seed catalogs until I was cool enough to shower and—"

"You got carried away. It hasn't been that long that I don't remember how you'd get when a new seed catalog came in the mail," Sam said. "See anything interesting in that one?" He nodded toward the discarded catalog.

Ruby smiled. "Nothing...and everything. You know how I am," she said, shrugging. "Now I really have to get ready. I have a hot date waiting for me."

"Anybody I know?" Sam asked, grinning.

"Probably," Ruby said. "He's tall, dark and handsome and in this house."

"Are you talking about me?"

Ruby hadn't heard Nick come in. He, too, had showered and was ready to go. Just how long had she been sitting there dreaming over that wish book? "If the shoe fits…" she said, shrugging and airily waving a hand. Then she hurried back to get ready for her date.

With Sam.

Too bad her cousin Nick had to tag along with them, too.

SAM SAT on the living room couch feeling more nervous and fidgety than a teenager waiting for his first date. Even after ten years of marriage, Ruby still had the ability to surprise him, and after her appearance in the red dress the other night, he was eager to see what she would turn up in today.

Even if his wife wore something he'd seen before, she would take his breath away. He was sure of it. But then, Sam supposed, he was slightly biased in her favor.

"I'm ready," Ruby called from the bedroom in the back of the house, and both Sam and Nick looked up as she entered.

Ruby was flushed and breathless and looked positively delicious. Her wavy red hair curled damply around her face, perfectly framing her peaches-and-cream skin, which was dusted with just a touch a brown-sugar freckles. She wore only a minimum of makeup, but she'd never needed much to improve her good looks: a little mascara, maybe, and a dab of lipstick. Of course, Sam had never cared if she wore none at all.

"Hoo-wee!" he drawled, rising. "You look good enough to eat." He eyed the bright yellow sundress that brought out the delicate color in Ruby's face, provided the perfect contrast to her coppery hair and showed off the gentle lines of her creamy white shoulders. He couldn't wait for another chance to dance so he could hold her in his arms and touch that velvety smooth expanse of skin the dress showed off so well.

"I second that, cuz," Nick said, getting to his feet as well. "Too bad there aren't two of you."

Ruby blushed. "Shoot, Nick. You've never been hard up for female company. I bet you'll be drawing stares from half the single girls in Jester."

"Hey!" Sam protested. "What about me? I'm your date, not Nick!"

Crooking her arm for Sam, Ruby laughed. "How well I know that, Slick. You are my date tonight, and I will probably have to beat your admirers off with a stick when they try to cut in."

Linking his arm through Ruby's, Sam grinned. "That's more like it. Looks like we all might have to defend your honor tonight, as well."

Laughing, the three of them hurried out to Ruby's SUV. Funny, Sam couldn't help thinking. The last time they'd gone to the Heartbreaker Saloon, he had believed Nick to be a rival, and now they were becoming friends. Could tonight be a turning point in his relationship with Ruby, as well?

RUBY HAD FORGOTTEN that today was Friday, and the small town of Jester was hopping—if you could call it that. There was certainly more activity downtown than she'd seen there in quite a long time. Cars and trucks were parked out in front of the Brimming Cup, open late for weekend business. In front of the Heartbreaker, a group of duded-up cowboys were unloading a shabby trailer proclaiming the owners to be the Rocky Gulch Band, suggesting that there would be live music tonight. And all the parking spaces along Mega-Bucks Boulevard were taken.

"Wow," Sam said. "I was here just a couple of hours ago, and this place was all but dead. What the hell happened?"

Nick laughed. "Friday night in Montana, man. Everybody is out for a good time."

"Well, I'm hungry," Ruby declared. "Sam, find us a parking place, and let's go before there's nothing left to eat. I'm starved, and I need to fortify myself so I can dance the night away to the music of the Rocky Gulch Band."

"Your wish is my command," Sam said, steering the SUV into a spot just vacated by a couple of kids who hardly looked old enough to date, much less drive. "Damn," he muttered. "Were we ever that young?"

"Unfortunately, yes," Ruby said, remembering the dances at Jester Public School when she was growing up. They always resulted in couples pairing off and making a trip to the local "lovers lane" down by the creek. "I bet I know where they're going." She couldn't help wishing that just maybe she and Sam would end up in a similar place later on tonight.

She looked at Sam and then down the street to a couple of teenagers who seemed unable to keep their hands off each other. She was so glad she'd not traveled the road that many of her classmates had, resulting in quickie marriages and kids too soon. She had gone all the way to Bozeman to college, had had a short career and had gotten away from Jester. At least for a few years. And had decided that she liked it better here.

"There you are," Honor called, beckoning from the bat-wing doors of the Heartbreaker. "I have the best news."

Ruby arched an eyebrow. She had spoken to Honor only yesterday, and her friend had been bemoaning her state of unweddedness. What kind of news could Honor possibly have that she hadn't had yesterday? Had she met a man in the last twenty-four hours?

Honor grabbed Ruby by the arm and dragged her inside. "Excuse us for a minute, Sam," she said, looking over her shoulder. "This is girl talk."

Sam nodded. "I'll get us a table. You know where to find me." He and Nick headed into the crowded dining area.

The saloon was definitely more lively tonight than it had been when she and Sam had come a few days before. Most of the tables were filled, and the jukebox was playing full blast, Ruby observed as she followed Honor to a slightly less noisy corner.

"What is it, Hon? Have you met someone?" It was the only reason Ruby could think of for Honor to be at the Heartbreaker Saloon, even in its new, improved state. Honor had always been quiet and shy. She was more likely to spend her Friday nights reading a book than hanging out at the tavern.

"I wish," Honor said, flicking her long blond hair out of her face with a freshly manicured hand. "But you've talked me into it. I'm going to take that trip." She held her hands up for Ruby to see. "Even got my nails done at the Crowning Glory to get ready for it.''

"What trip?'' Ruby remembered discussing the fact that Honor might need a change of scene, but she definitely did not remember twisting her friend's arm and telling her to go anywhere.

"I'm going to go around the world. I've booked the trip. I'm really going to do it!'' she explained excitedly. "I'm going to shop, see the sights and maybe, just maybe, meet Mr. Right,'' Honor declared, her gray eyes glowing with excitement.

Ruby certainly wished her friend luck, but she wondered what would happen to their store if both of them were no longer involved. "What about—''

"The Mercantile? I've got it all figured out.'' Honor paused to take a breath, then went on in a rush. "Valerie Simms is looking for something a little more challenging than waiting tables at the Brimming Cup. I thought we could bring her in and teach her the ropes at the store, and she could manage it. She and baby Max can move into the apartment upstairs. That way she'd be close enough to keep an eye on the baby, too.''

"Well, you certainly have it all figured out, don't you, Honor?'' Ruby said, her head swimming with all that her friend had just told her. "Are you sure that Valerie is up to it?''

"I won't be gone forever, and there are other employees there who know what's going on. Most of the time the place practically runs itself.'' Honor smiled. "Valerie will be fine.''

"But won't the other ladies feel slighted if they're passed over for the job?''

"Already checked. Nobody wants the responsibility. Most of our employees have families and want to be able to go home to them at the end of the day.'' Honor waved to someone who had just come in. ''This is the perfect thing for Valerie.''

Ruby glanced through the crowded saloon to see what had happened to Sam and Nick. ''Well,'' she said slowly, ''I guess it wouldn't hurt to give it a try. And there's no sense in letting that apartment sit empty when Valerie could put it to good use.''

And it would be a good reason to have Sam move all his belongings out to the farm for good. Then maybe she wouldn't worry so much about him packing up and leaving. ''All right, Hon. You do it. Now, I've got to go. I have two dates waiting for me.''

''Two dates?'' Honor echoed. ''Some people have all the luck.''

''Hey,'' Ruby said, having had a sudden stroke of inspiration. ''Why don't you join us? You haven't met my cousin Nick yet.''

''I guess I can,'' Honor replied slowly. ''I only came over to the Heartbreaker to tell you my decision. Sam told me you were coming here when he passed through the store earlier. I'll have to call my folks and tell them not to expect me.''

''You do that, and I'll go find Sam and Nick.'' And, Ruby couldn't help thinking, if she played her cards right, Nick and Honor would hit it off, and there would be no need for her to take that trip.

Ruby watched as Honor threaded her way through the crowd to the pay phone on the other side of the room. She really would like a happy ending for her long-time friend. And herself, as well.

But if she didn't hurry up and pay attention to the man who'd brought her, that would never happen. She scanned the noisy room and finally located the table where Sam and Nick were seated. Ruby drew a deep breath and hurried over.

Now she just had to figure out how to orchestrate a happy ending for herself.

The sooner the better.

Tonight would work just fine, as far as she was concerned.

SAM AND RUBY SWAYED to the soft strains of a ballad played by the Rocky Gulch Band. The group wasn't very good, but what they lacked in talent they made up for in enthusiasm. And Sam wanted to dance as an excuse to get Ruby into his arms.

These few moments had to sustain him until he could convince his wife that he wasn't going to leave her again. They had to hold him until Ruby would finally allow him back into her bed as well as her home.

"Damn, you feel good in my arms," he murmured, breathing in the sweet, fruity scent of her perfume as he caressed her silky, smooth shoulders.

"I've missed this," she whispered back, her warm breath so close to his ear sending shivers of anticipation running up and down Sam's spine.

"I've missed you," Sam replied huskily, brushing coppery hair away from one milk-white ear. He felt a tingling in his groin, and wondered how he'd disguise it when he was holding Ruby so close. He wanted so much to make love to her, but he didn't want to push her, even if waiting and holding back was like living in his own private hell.

Sam glanced up and noticed that Dev had stepped

up to the stage and was whispering something to the band. He wondered what that was all about.

His question was answered quickly enough as the band ended the slow song.

"I hate to do this to y'all," the singer said, "but Dev here says the weather bureau has issued a severe storm warning. There's a big line of thunderstorms heading straight for us, and he figured it would be best if everybody headed on home before the storms hit." He shrugged and lifted his guitar strap over his head. "So I reckon that was the last song. G'night, folks! Drive safe, y'hear?"

Sam shouted a silent cheer. That was as good a reason as any to make their excuses and head home. And if Dev Devlin thought the storm front was bad enough to consider closing down the Heartbreaker, then it wasn't an ordinary storm front. He looked down at Ruby, whose brows were knitted with concern. She'd never liked thunderstorms. "I reckon we'd best get on home, sugar," he said.

"I suppose so," Ruby agreed. "Let's round up Nick and get going."

"Somebody mention my name?"

Sam turned to see Nick and Honor coming up behind them. "Yeah. Looks like we're going to have to call it a night."

"Okay." Nick stepped back and looked down at Honor. "Can we take you home?" he asked.

Ruby arched an eyebrow and gave Sam one of those telling looks. Had she been matchmaking? Sam wondered.

Honor shook her head. "Thanks, but no. I live just around the corner on Big Draw Drive. I can walk."

"We don't mind dropping you off," Sam offered.

"It's late and there are a lot of strangers out on the street tonight. Wouldn't want anything to happen to you."

Honor looked not at Sam, but at Nick. "Well, I guess so. I wouldn't want to worry you," she said softly. "Thank you. I'd appreciate a lift."

And Sam would appreciate them getting on with it. With the approaching storm, he'd finally been presented with a surefire way to get Ruby into his bed. She had always been terrified of storms and a severe one was guaranteed to send her running, cowering, into the shelter of his arms.

All he had to do was get them all home before that storm hit.

Chapter Thirteen

Ruby watched the lightning flickering in the distance with growing apprehension. She wasn't so much worried about the approaching storm as she was that she and Sam wouldn't reach home before it hit. She'd long since gotten over her fear of storms themselves, but she did have a healthy respect for the damage they could do.

She'd seen a tornado come tearing across the plains toward her family's ranch when she was a child, and she'd never forgotten that awesome sight. Though no humans had been injured in that particular storm, it had decimated a herd of cattle, ripped trees right out of the ground and left several outbuildings looking like nothing more than a pile of matchsticks. A sight like that could imprint itself indelibly on a child's psyche.

She shuddered as she remembered.

Sam reached over and patted her knee, making her shiver with anticipation. And not of the storm. "It's okay, Ruby. We'll be home well before the storm hits."

Of course, Sam had no way of knowing that she'd conquered her fear of storms during the time he'd been overseas and she'd been living alone in the apartment above the Mercantile. But still, Ruby liked the idea that Sam wanted to protect her.

And this storm was giving her the perfect opportunity to let Sam back into her bed where he belonged without either one of them having to admit they'd made a mistake. She was pretty sure they both understood that by now.

"Turn on the radio. Let's hear the weather report," Nick suggested from the back seat.

"Good idea." Sam switched on the radio and staticky music filled the air.

"Damn. Why aren't they giving the report?" Nick muttered.

"Probably because it's not that bad," Ruby suggested. "They only give complete coverage if storms are expected to be really dangerous."

"Then why did Dev send us all home?" Nick fumed. "I was enjoying myself."

"I expect I know," Sam said. "Dev's got a new wife. Maybe he was looking for an excuse to close up early and go home to Amanda."

"Maybe so," Nick grumbled. "But the man stands to lose my repeat business if he keeps doing that," he added sourly. "Besides, Roy could keep things open if Dev went home."

Ruby laughed. "Nick Folger, you are going home to South Dakota in another week. I think Dev will be able to keep the wolf from his door without you here." And she completely understood why Dev wanted to get home to Amanda. Maybe it wasn't a very dangerous storm, but it was as good an excuse as any to crawl into bed with someone you loved.

She was planning on using a very similar excuse herself.

"Sam, do you suppose you could manage to drive a little faster?" Ruby asked. She had always hated speeding in the fast, low-slung Corvette, but in the SUV it was okay. After all, she had a reason to hurry home.

"Don't worry, Ruby, darlin'. I won't let the storm beat us to the house," Sam said as he pressed on the gas and the SUV surged forward.

That wasn't what Ruby was worried about.

She was afraid the storm would pass them by, and she'd lose her excuse.

Not that she'd let on to Sam.

Yet.

"WELL, IT LOOKS LIKE it's going to pass us by," Sam said, glancing at the retreating storm in the distance and trying to conceal his disappointment as he stepped out of the car. The air outside was still thick with humidity, though, so maybe there was a slim chance that another storm might head their way later.

A guy could hope.

Funny how, considering her storm phobia, Ruby didn't look the least bit relieved, Sam thought as he escorted her, hand at the small of her bare back, up the path to the house. A slight frown furrowed her alabaster brow as the breeze taunted them with the promise of rain—a promise it might not keep.

Sam drew in a deep breath. Was that the scent of rain he detected in the sultry air?

"Yeah," Ruby said, sounding disappointed. "We could use the rain, though." She let out a low sigh and pushed open the front door.

Looking for any excuse to touch her, Sam reached around her and flipped on the light. "No sense in you tripping on something and hurting yourself," he said, brushing his hand against her creamy shoulder, shown off to tempting advantage by the yellow dress. Then he wondered what might have happened if Ruby had tripped.

He could have picked her up and carried her to her bed. His bed. Their bed.

He might have been able to put an end to this ridiculous charade once and for all.

Damn. Why had he been so gallant?

The air inside the house was stuffy and warm, and Sam stopped to push open a window in the living room. "If it does rain, it won't come in under the porch," he said, looking for something, anything, to keep Ruby from retreating alone into her bedroom quite so soon.

"I suppose," she murmured, punctuating her answer with a low sigh. "I guess I should open one in the bedroom, too." She wandered slowly across the living room, as if she didn't quite know where she was going or what she was going to do.

What was wrong with the woman? "Ruby, don't you feel well?"

"Just tired, Sam," she said, and she really did sound weary.

Why was he reading more into everything than was actually there? Was he reading between the lines or was he merely guilty of wishful thinking? Sam reached for Ruby's hand and pulled her to him.

"Is something on your mind, Ruby?" he asked, holding her gently by her upper arms. He caressed and massaged her creamy soft skin, and Ruby seemed

to tremble in response. Sam was determined to give
her every chance to invite him into her bed. But as
the minutes ticked slowly by, his chances seemed increasingly slim.

Why had he made that stupid, foolhardy promise
not to push her?

Ruby shook her head. "I'm fine. Just tired. It's
been a long day. I think I'll just go on to bed."

Alone, dammit, Sam couldn't help thinking. When
was the blasted impasse going to come to an end?
When was Ruby going to stop testing and accept that
he was here to stay?

He released her and watched as she slowly turned
away. He was gonna need another cold shower tonight, that was for sure. He'd taken too many lately,
and it hadn't been because of the hot, sticky air in the
house.

It was because of Ruby's decidedly cold shoulder.

RUBY CLOSED THE BEDROOM door, using every bit of
restraint she possessed to keep from slamming it. If
she'd had something to kick, she would have; she was
so angry with herself! Why couldn't she just swallow
her pride and tell Sam that she was ready to end their
separation?

It was plain as day that Sam wanted her back. And
ever since Ruby had learned the real reason her husband had gone out on that mission that night she'd
called to tell him about winning part of the lottery,
she was feeling more than a little guilty for not having
given him a chance to explain before she'd jumped
to all the wrong conclusions.

She unzipped her dress, kicked off her shoes,
maybe a little more forcefully than necessary, and

plopped down prone on the bed. Balling up her fists, she pounded on the soft, giving mattress. It wasn't as satisfactory as punching a wall, but it would have to do. She'd made her bed and here she was lying in it. Alone.

Now she just had to figure out how to get out of it.

As the storm moved off and the flickers of lightning outside her bedroom window grew dimmer, she made her decision.

Tonight would be the night, she decided. Storm or no storm.

SAM WRESTLED his bedroom window up and stood, naked and damp, in the open expanse, hoping to catch even a hint of the frail, humid breeze. He stared off into the darkness, which was unrelieved by lights or stars or the slightest flash of lightning. A shower had cooled him off, but it had done nothing to douse his burning desire for his wife.

His loins raged with a fire that could only be eased by Ruby. In his bed. Beneath him.

A slight breath of wind stirred the sheer curtains and brought with it the suggestion of impending rain. Sam could smell it in the air, but he shrugged. The storm had already passed. He could not count on another one to send Ruby running into his arms. And besides, rain or not, she would come to him when she came to him. He tried to be philosophical about it, but he was rapidly running out of patience.

A man could stand only so much waiting.

He turned slowly to the bed and stretched out on top of the covers. He was too hot and bothered to sleep, and at least this way he'd be able to take advantage of what little breeze meandered his way.

MIDNIGHT.

The bold, red LED display on the alarm clock seemed to scream at her, but the old house was as still and silent as it normally was at night.

Ruby lay quietly in her bed, listening to sounds of the house settling. An occasional breeze fluttered the sheers on the window, but otherwise the night was still as a tomb.

She shuddered at the thought.

Though the storm had apparently passed them by, the stars had not reappeared in the sky, suggesting that clouds still covered its infinite expanse.

Why had she needed a storm, anyway?

All she had to do was knock on Sam's door, and she had no doubt that he'd let her in. Sam had promised to wait until she was ready, and he was an officer and a gentleman, medical retirement or not. He would not break his word.

It was all up to her.

She was ready to move forward, and she realized now she was the only one who could set them on the right path.

Ruby yanked the cord on the bedside lamp and pushed herself up out of the tangled sheets. As quietly as she could, she slid to the floor and tiptoed to her bureau. In the top drawer was the nightgown—if you could call that tiny scrap of peach-colored silk a nightgown—that she'd planned to wear for Sam's homecoming.

If she were going to seduce her husband, it was going to take something a little more attractive than

Sam's old T-shirt that she'd taken to wearing to sleep in when he'd gone overseas. Of course, Sam had made it perfectly clear that no seduction would be necessary. Still, Ruby felt she had to make the effort.

She pulled the worn and faded T-shirt over her head and slipped into the silken gown. How smooth and weightless it felt against her bare skin. Knowing how quickly Sam would pull it over her head and fling it away, she put it on anyway.

How wonderful his hands would feel against her breasts— Ruby's breath caught in her throat.

Why was she standing here? Why was she imagining what might happen when all she had to do was walk down the hall and experience the real thing?

She drew in a deep breath, squared her shoulders and pushed open the bedroom door.

The rest was up to Sam.

SAM JERKED UP, instantly alert, at the sound of something he couldn't quite identify. He held his breath as he tuned out the creaking of the old house and focused in on the noise he'd thought he heard.

There it was again.

Someone or something was outside in the hall. And no one who belonged here had any reason for stealth. If someone was creeping through the house, he was up to no good.

The security lamp from the barn sent a path of light across the floor, straight to the door. As Sam crept toward it, he could clearly see the knob turn.

The mechanism clicked free with a quiet snick, and the door pushed inward. Sam waited, breath bated, behind the door. Waited, tense and ready, until whoever was trying to come in showed himself and gave him a chance to grab him.

The door slowly creaked open and a shadowy figure, shrouded in the darkness, stepped inside. Another moment and Sam would grab him.

"Kee-yah!" Sam shouted as he lunged for the intruder and grabbed him around the neck.

A soft silky neck, he realized as his victim shrieked. A neck that was much too slender and velvety smooth to be that of a man.

Sam abruptly let go. "What the hell? Ruby?"

The shadow let out a low, shaky and decidedly feminine breath. "Next time I guess I'll knock first," she said dryly.

"Ruby Melissa Albright Cade! What the hell are you doing sneaking into my room like this?" Sam demanded as he flipped on the overhead light.

Ruby blinked at the sudden illumination. "I was trying to surprise you," she said, rubbing her throat with a trembling hand. A red mark showed where he had grabbed her, and Sam wanted—no, needed—to kiss the mark away. "This was not exactly what I had in mind."

Sam brushed Ruby's hand away from the angry marks on her throat. "Oh, God, Ruby. Did I do that? I am so sorry!"

"It's all right, Sam. I guess I was asking for it." She wound her arms around his neck, and Sam was suddenly, acutely aware that he was naked. And Ruby was nearly so, wrapped in a piece of silk that was only slightly larger than a handkerchief.

"I guess I'll have to kiss it and make it better," Sam murmured huskily, lowering his face to Ruby's exquisite, delicate throat.

"You do that, Sam," Ruby replied softly, sultrily as Sam's lips touched her silken skin. "And then will you take me to bed?"

Sam's breath caught. "Do you have to ask?"

She shook her head. "No, I didn't think so," she answered breathlessly. "But I know you've been waiting for the proper invitation."

"Hoo-ah!" Sam cheered. "I accept." He lifted her into his arms and carried her, light as a feather, to the bed.

As he lowered her to the top of the covers, she murmured the words he was beginning to think he'd never hear. "Sam, I am so sorry that I let that misunderstanding come between us. Will you ever be able to forgive me?"

He settled down beside her, trying to temper his excitement. "Of course I can. But, darlin'," he drawled. "It would be a hell of a lot easier if you didn't have that silly nightgown comin' between you and me."

Ruby grinned, then slowly and seductively began to peel the nightgown off in a striptease that was moving much too slowly.

Sam grabbed the offending piece of silk and snatched it the rest of the way off, and Ruby, in all her naked glory, sat perched on his bed in front of him.

As a loud clap of thunder sounded, followed by a blinding flash of lightning, Sam closed the short distance between them. He felt Ruby's warm, damp skin against his, and he knew he'd found heaven on earth.

Then, as he lowered himself over her, the power went out.

Ruby didn't care that the lights were out, that thunder was crashing and lightning flashing all around her. So powerful was her urgent desire for Sam, for the fulfillment that only he could bring, that she scarcely heard anything save the beating of their hearts in tandem and the sound of their breathing as she and Sam finally came together.

He covered her willing body, kneed her legs apart and surged into her so quickly that it made Ruby gasp as they became one.

Sam paused and, braced by his arms, hovered above her. "Are you all right, Ruby?" he asked, obviously trying so hard to hold back that he trembled with the effort. "I want so much to make this night perfect for you, but I…it's been…so long."

Ruby smiled and raised her head to place a soft kiss on Sam's mouth. Tendrils of desire wound their way from her throbbing center through her body to her heart. "It's all right, Sam. I want you so much. And we have all night."

"Yes, we do, darlin'," Sam murmured. "And I promise I will make it up to you the second time around."

Ruby laughed softly, raised her hips and moved seductively beneath his body, making him jump reflexively inside her. Sighing with satisfaction, she trailed one hand down his bumpy spine, smiling as she felt gooseflesh form on his skin. That had always driven Sam wild, and Ruby loved the power she felt when it did. "Go on, Sam. Please. It's been just as long for me."

He pushed deep inside her and rocked back and forth, back and forth, surging more powerfully each time, like wave after wave pounding a sandy white beach. A kaleidoscope of light and sound and emotion overwhelmed Ruby, and she rode to the crest of each wave of passion and sensation with an ecstasy more fierce and powerful than the storm outside.

She felt Sam contract within her, and Ruby anticipated his slight gasp of breath an instant before he made it. Then, with a triumphant cry of pleasure, he emptied himself into her. Quickly following him to completion, she tumbled, swirling head over heels over the brink with her own satisfied cry of completion.

This was the way it always had been.

This was as it should ever be.

SATED FOR NOW, Sam caressed Ruby's skin, still damp from their lovemaking, as she nestled against him in the crook of his arm, her head on his chest. He could feel the soft rhythm of her heartbeat against him as she lay in his arms, and everything seemed right with the world.

"I love you, Ruby." He kissed the top of her tousled head and smiled as she snuggled closer, murmuring something he could not understand and really didn't care that he didn't.

"Ruby, are you awake?"

She didn't answer, but the soft, even sound of her breathing suggested she was fast asleep.

"That's so like you, Ruby, my beautiful, priceless gem. Always giving, and me always taking," he whispered. He kissed her again. "But I will make it up to you," he promised. "If not tonight, then tomorrow. It's about time that I learned to give as much as you have."

He lay there for a long, long time, listening to the sound of the departing storm and the quiet, even rhythm of Ruby's breathing. Nothing mattered to him except this beautiful, loving woman who finally lay so peacefully, so trustingly in his arms.

Sam hadn't realized how much she'd sacrificed, how much she'd given to him until now, and he wondered about his sudden stroke of clarity.

Had he really been the taker in their marriage? Had he been wrong to put his career first and his wife second? Obviously, Ruby had felt that way. And she'd never said a word. Until now.

Not until she'd believed that he'd betrayed her one time too many. And he'd been a clueless idiot until the day he'd received that letter from her lawyer.

Chapter Fourteen

Ruby fitfully brushed at the thing fluttering lightly against her cheek as she roused slowly from a deep, restful sleep. Whatever it was brushed her again, and Ruby slowly opened her eyes.

"Good mornin', darlin'," Sam drawled, from slightly above her. He was propped up on one elbow, a half smile on his handsome face, teasing her cheek with a tangled lock of her hair.

"Morning," she murmured, stretching languidly as she slowly came awake. The light coming through the sheer curtains on the window was dim, diffused, making colors barely distinguishable as night gave way to morning. "What are you doing?" she asked sleepily. "What time is it, anyway?"

"Early," Sam said. "Time for me to start making good on my promises, darlin'," he added. "You went to sleep on me last night," he said, smiling.

"Oh, Sam. I'm so s—"

Sam stopped her apology with a touch of his fingertips against her mouth. "Hush now. I know you haven't been sleeping so well, so I let you. We have the rest of our lives together to finish this. One day's delay won't much matter in the scheme of things."

A rush of love and joy threatened to overwhelm her, and Ruby blinked back the hot tears that flooded her eyes. She knew Sam would never understand tears at a time like this, so she did the first thing she could think of to keep them from falling. She reached up and drew his dear, handsome face, scratchy with morning stubble, down to hers. "I love you so much, Sam," she whispered, and then she kissed him.

As Ruby knew he would, Sam circled her with his arms. She wrapped her own around him, holding him tightly as if she'd never let go. As their bodies performed the familiar dance and became one, only a single thought echoed in her brain.

How could she ever have considered facing the rest of her life without Sam?

"I RECKON WE'D BEST get moving, darlin'," Sam whispered into Ruby's ear later, after they'd finished and lay sated in each other's arms. He loved the way Ruby felt when he held her, but they did have a farm to run, the sun had long since risen, and Nick would show up in the kitchen sooner or later and want breakfast.

"Oh my gosh," Ruby exclaimed, pushing herself up with a jerk. "Nick! What will he think?"

Sam laughed. "He'll think we've been doing exactly what we've been doing," he said, then shrugged.

Ruby blushed, her creamy face going from white to rosy-pink in seconds.

"Why should he care? We're married, and we've only been doing what married couples all over the world do." Sam swung his legs over the edge of the bed. "Last one up has to wait on the shower." Then he got up and headed for the bathroom, leaving Ruby to dress. Or not.

Or join him in the shower to save time.

Of course, Sam knew there was a chance Ruby wouldn't accept his unspoken invitation. She might not be quite as ready to leap back into their old, familiar habits as he was. Only time would tell.

Sam pulled open the shower curtain and adjusted the spray while he waited for the water to get hot. He'd have to talk to Nick about redoing this bathroom, he thought. It would be great to have one of those whirlpool baths, big enough for two. It would be great for his injured knee. And for their love life, as well.

He stepped into the shower and pulled the curtains shut behind him. The water was hot and steamy and the stinging spray was just what he needed to finally shake off the languor of their morning of lovemaking. He began to wash, and only half noticed when Ruby drew the curtain open and stepped inside.

He felt first a brief rush of cool air, and then the impression of her perfect breasts against his back as she pressed herself to him. "Help, call 9-1-1! There's an intruder in my shower," he teased as he turned his soapy wet body around in Ruby's arms to face her.

She laughed. "There's no such thing as sophisticated as 9-1-1 way out here," she said. "You'd have to call Luke McNeil, and this bathtub is not big enough for the three of us." She slid her hands slowly and seductively up Sam's wet and soapy chest. "But it's been much too long since I've had my back scrubbed."

"Well, don't I know that," Sam drawled, and he soaped up one of Ruby's bath scrubbies and began to spread frothy, foamy bubbles all over her slender white back.

"Mmm," Ruby murmured with obvious pleasure, shifting her shoulders to direct Sam's ministrations. "I could stay here all day."

"I'm sure we could, but having Nick standin' outside, poundin' on the door and yelling at us to hurry can sure be distractin'."

Ruby grabbed the scrubby from Sam and tossed it at him. "Well, go then. You've had plenty of time to get clean. And Petunia and the piglets don't care whether you've shaved or not," she said.

Sam pulled her to him and rubbed his bristly cheek against hers. "What about you, sugar?"

"I'll be fine," Ruby said primly. "Just as long as a you've shaved by bedtime." She pushed him away. "Now go. My beautiful new kitchen is waiting."

SAM WAS NOWHERE to be seen when Ruby finally made her way into the makeshift kitchen in the dining room. Nick looked up from his coffee as she entered, and grinned knowingly. Why she felt her face warm with an embarrassing blush, Ruby didn't know, but blush she did. "What did Sam tell you?" she managed to ask as she tried to push her embarrassment aside.

"Nothing," Nick said as he watched her over the brim of his coffee mug. "Didn't have to."

Still feeling awkward about what her cousin had figured out, Ruby busied herself with her own coffee. She carefully kept her back to him as she poured. Thank goodness for automatic coffeemakers.

"You're running short of milk, and cereal's about gone," Nick said from behind Ruby's back. "Good news, though. Your kitchen should be finished and ready to go by the end of the day. And I'll be able to go home.''

Amazed that the wreck of a room could be transformed so quickly, Ruby turned. ''So soon? How can you possibly…?''

Nick pushed himself up out of his chair. ''I'll be heading on out in a day or so,'' he said. ''No matter what you say. You two don't need me around while you're getting reacquainted.''

''We love having you here,'' Ruby protested.

''Speak for yourself, woman,'' Sam said, coming in through the kitchen.

She was about to object to Sam's statement, but then noticed the grin on his face. ''That was rude,'' she couldn't resist stating.

''Nick knows I'm kidding,'' Sam said, taking her into his arms and kissing her possessively. It felt so great to have his arms around her, but Sam knew that if they kept this up they'd never get anything done around the farm. He let go of her and turned to Nick. ''Seriously, man. I appreciate all you've done for Ruby while I was away.''

''No big deal,'' Nick said, shaking his head and backing away. ''Ruby's family. We might not see each other very often, but we come when we're needed. We do for each other.''

That was quite a speech coming from Ruby's usually taciturn cousin, but Sam understood and appreciated the sentiment. ''And you know we'll do anything we can for you, if you need us.''

''I know that,'' Nick said, suddenly turning his head toward the window. ''I think I hear a truck coming.'' He hurried outside to investigate.

"Your cousin is a good man," Sam told Ruby. They watched through the window as Nick strode out to greet the craftsman who would help make Ruby's kitchen a dream come true.

"Yes, he is," Ruby agreed. "But a cousin in the hand is not the same as a husband in the bed. I love you, Sam," she said, turning back to face him. "I'm so glad we've been able to work through our problems."

"Amen to that, sugar," Sam said. He kissed her lingeringly even though he knew the kiss could lead to nothing else. Right now.

Ruby turned quickly and pulled out of Sam's embrace at the sharp sound of footsteps, then laughed as Oscar stepped daintily into the dining room from the kitchen and oinked indignantly. "How did you get in here?" she asked as the pig trotted up to her.

"That back door hasn't been closing properly since we've been working in the kitchen. I bet the dampness from last night's storm kept it from shutting when Nick went out."

Ruby bent down to look at the piglet, which was inquisitively rooting around the legs of the dining room table. Oscar stopped his exploration of his surroundings and looked up at her. "Did he eat?" she asked.

"I fed the other pigs, but Oscar wasn't around," Sam said. "He's the only one who's still small enough to slip under the fence rails."

"Well, I'll go give him some piggy chow while you eat. You are hungry, aren't you?"

"Only for you, darlin'. Only for you." Sam could

tell exactly when Ruby went all soft and mushy inside. Man, he thought, it was going to be a long time until tonight.

"MAN, I DIDN'T THINK we were going to make it," Sam said as he stood back and admired the finished kitchen. "It sure was a lot of work to accomplish in one day."

"Where there's a will, there's a way," Nick said. "And getting everything coordinated so that it all comes together is the hardest part."

"Yeah, I bet it is. Especially when you have to order everything from so far away." That was another reason Sam had never considered coming out here to Montana to stay. But in spite of that, he'd learned to appreciate the quiet and serenity he'd found out here on the farm. And of course, he loved Ruby. That was a hell of an incentive to hang around.

If Ruby loved this place, then he could learn to love it, too.

"Yeah," Nick said. "We just have to do a little cleanup, and we can call Ruby in for the unveiling."

"Sending her into town and out of our hair was a stroke of inspiration," Sam said. "Otherwise she'd be here underfoot now."

Nick snorted, then stepped back as well, surveying the completed project. "I don't know how long she'll stay gone with that wild-goose chase you sent her on."

Sam chuckled. "Yeah. I just hope she won't be spitting mad when she finds out we didn't really need that box of finishing nails, but it kept her out of our way. How did you know they wouldn't have any on hand at Faulkner's Hardware?"

"Called first," Nick said, grinning. "If they'd had

them, I'd have just thought of something else they wouldn't be likely to have.''

"As long as Ruby had to go to Pine Run to get them," Sam concluded. That was probably the longest conversation he'd ever had with Nick, he thought as they settled into a comfortable silence. He couldn't wait to see the expression on Ruby's face when she saw the finished project.

Sam glanced at the clock on the newly installed microwave oven. Was it really nearly seven?

Ruby should have been back hours ago. Where in the hell was she?

THE TEMPTING AROMA of fried chicken taunted Ruby all the way back from Pine Run. She'd finally located the finishing nails Nick needed, then had decided to make the best of her trip to Pine Run and had done some other errands while she was there. Now it was late, and she was tired and hungry, so she'd stopped at the fast-food chicken place on the way out of town and purchased a bucket and all the fixings for dinner.

She parked in front of the house and grabbed the red-and-white bucket of chicken and the bag of extras off the seat next to her and headed up the path to the house.

Then she looked up to see Sam and Nick grinning at her from the front porch. "What has you two looking so pleased with yourselves?" she called as she hurried up the walk.

"Oh, nothing much," Sam said, feigning an innocent expression as he took the bucket of chicken out of her hands and Nick took the bag. Come to think of it, Nick was looking pretty smug himself.

"Hurry up. You've got a couple of starving men

on your hands,'' Nick said as Ruby reached the foot of the steps.

Nick opened the front door with a flourish, and Sam escorted her inside. ''Here, I'll put this stuff on the dining room table and you can get the iced tea from the refrigerator,'' Sam said.

''Why don't you fetch the tea, and I'll get the food ready?'' Ruby said. ''I think I have some paper plates in the buffet cabinet.'' She stopped short.

The formal dining room table was spread with a white linen tablecloth and set with her best china, including the crystal stemware that Sam had sent her from one of his trips to Germany. ''What's...going on?'' Then it dawned on her, and Ruby let out a whoop of joy. She dropped her pocket book on the floor and rushed to the kitchen, pausing on the tips of her toes in the doorway.

''It's finished! Hoo-yah!'' she cheered, giving her own imitation of Sam's military cry.

''Just for you, cuz,'' Nick said, grinning.

''You like?'' Sam said.

''What's not to like?'' Ruby asked as she took in all the details of the sparkling new kitchen, from the polished, terra-cotta tile floor to the gleaming stainless steel appliances. The countertops gleamed, and the guys had even put up the curtains she'd made.

''I love it!'' Ruby started across the floor to get the iced tea out of the refrigerator, but Nick pulled her back.

''You can look, but don't touch,'' he said. ''The grout has to set before we can walk on the floor. Wait till morning.''

''But what will we drink?''

Sam took her by the upper arms and turned her

around to face the table. There in a champagne bucket they'd seldom used was a bottle of champagne, chilling. "Thought we might need this for our little celebration."

"Where did— I'm…I'm stunned. Speechless," Ruby said, her heart skipping a beat. "Oh, you guys."

"Bought it in Pine Run last week," Sam said. "I hoped to have a use for it sooner or later."

Ruby blushed, realizing what celebration Sam had probably bought it for.

"Sit. Eat," Nick demanded, apparently not noticing her flushed face. "I know you and Sam have better things to do than have me hanging around." He grinned. "I'll just eat and then leave you two alone. I figure you have some private celebrating to do."

"You don't have to leave, Nick," Ruby said, her words sounding insincere, even to herself.

"Yeah, right," Nick said. "Sam and I might have buried the hatchet, but he'll bury one in me if I overstay my welcome."

"Got that in one," Sam said, uncorking the champagne with a gentle pop. He poured the foaming beverage into three glasses, then lifted his in a toast.

"To Nick, who made this happen," he said.

Ruby lifted hers. "May he find as much happiness as we have." She brought her glass to her lips, enjoying the feeling of the effervescent bubbles beneath her nose before she sipped.

Nick lifted his glass to his lips and drank. "I'll be outta here first thing in the morning. I've got a business to get off the ground."

Sam lifted his own glass. "To Nick and his new undertaking. May it be successful."

"To Nick," Ruby echoed.

Nick just smiled.

LATER THAT NIGHT, as a gentle, cooling breeze blew in the open window, Sam held Ruby nestled in his arms. The soft glow of one flickering, scented candle allowed him to gaze down at her lithe, slender body, pressed against his. He couldn't believe how happy he was. How happy this one lovely woman had made him.

There had been a time when he'd selfishly believed that nothing could beat the adrenaline rush and excitement of leaping from a plane and landing on his feet in the middle of a dangerous situation. Now here he was, cradling the woman he loved in his arms, looking forward to the rest of his life with her. On a farm—a farm, for God's sake—and he was loving it.

Sam kissed the top of Ruby's tousled head, her fine curly hair still damp from their lovemaking. How could any man prefer jumping out of airplanes to this?

How could he have ever been so damned stupid to risk losing it all?

"You know what, Sam?" Ruby murmured sleepily, shifting in his arms.

"Hmm?" he answered quietly. He hadn't realized that Ruby was still awake.

"I think we should celebrate," she said softly, her warm breath fanning his chest and setting the banked fire inside him ablaze again.

"I thought we already had," Sam said. "But I'm game for another go at it."

Ruby chuckled, doing nothing to dampen his ardor. "I'm sure you are," she said dryly as she slid her fingers seductively along his sensitive skin and tangled them in the hair on his chest. "But I meant with our friends. We should have a party."

"Ah, I see," Sam concluded. "You want to show off your new kitchen and make all your friends insanely jealous."

Ruby pushed herself up on her elbow and looked down at Sam in the flickering candlelight. "No, silly. I want to show off my wonderful old husband. And all my friends already are green with envy."

Sam could see the teasing smile on her face and knew he had to do something about it. "I like the 'wonderful' part," he said as he quickly grabbed her and pushed her back down on the sheets, pinning her hands to the mattress with his. "But I take offense at being called old," he growled.

"What are you going to do? Challenge me to a duel?" Ruby teased. "Call me out at dawn?"

"No, woman," Sam said, covering her with his body. "But I'll show you that there is still plenty of life in this ole Georgia boy."

Ruby laughed, her body vibrating beneath him, making him want her more. "And just how are you going to do that?"

"Oh, I can think of something," he said, lowering his face to squelch Ruby's teasing smirk.

"Show me," Ruby demanded, her lips puckered below his.

Sam kissed her. And then he showed her.

Almost until dawn.

Chapter Fifteen

"This is so exciting," Gwen Tanner said as she made her way through the mudroom to the kitchen. Her arms were ladened with cardboard cake boxes that she could barely see over, and Sam hastened to relieve her of her burden. She stood in the middle of the kitchen, her greatly pregnant condition impossible to hide, and looked around.

Sam shot Ruby an I-told-you-so look, and Ruby winked back at him as Gwen nodded approvingly.

"I love it," Gwen exclaimed, her hands clasped together above her protruding stomach. "It's almost as good as mine."

"Well, I don't do quite the same amount of cooking as you do," Ruby said. "But I couldn't resist the cooktop range. Even if I had to get Nick to install a generator for when the power goes out."

"Nick did what?" Sam asked absently, eyeing the goodies Gwen had brought.

"Installed a generator," Ruby answered. "I bet a generator would come in handy for the boarding-house, too."

Gwen looked at Sam, a gleam of anticipation in her green eyes. "I've spent so much money on the rest of the house and getting ready for the babies, but I never even thought about something to keep everything working. And I'll need it when the babies come.''

"Nick went back to Rapid City," Sam said. ''But I can tell you where to get one and who around here can put it in for you," he offered. "Before he left, Nick gave me a list of the people he used.''

"Oh, yes," Gwen exclaimed. "That would be great. When the babies come, it will be a lot easier if I don't have to worry about keeping them comfortable and warm.''

She smiled a watery smile, then clapped her hands together briskly in a businesslike manner. "Now, let's get this food set out. If you don't stop fooling around, your guests will start arriving and you won't be ready for them.''

Ruby smiled. She had a we're-not-getting-divorced party to prepare for, and time was ticking away.

SAM STABBED THE LAST of the tiki torches into the ground and stepped back to survey his handiwork. It was too early to light them, but they were all ready for later. He couldn't have imagined that a simple get-together would have taken as much work and as many trips to Pine Run for supplies, but the nights with Ruby had been worth all the extra effort.

On top of all that, he had stripped the peeling paint off the ranch house and repainted the place while Ruby enjoyed the task of decorating her new kitchen and planning the party with Gwen. Somehow, Sam thought, Ruby got the better part of the deal.

Still, he enjoyed the thought of sharing their good news with their friends, even if everybody in town already knew about it. He wondered if that busybody Wyla Thorne would show up and if they'd find themselves news in the *Pine Run Plain Talker* again. He still hadn't been able to prove definitively that Wyla had been responsible for all the tidbits that kept showing up in the newspaper, but he'd bank on it. If he had to.

The breeze shifted, bringing with it the smoky scent of real Southern-style barbecue. Sam had insisted on it, and he'd been in charge of slow cooking the pig—not one of theirs, heaven forbid!—and making sure it was done right. Even if he and Ruby had felt they needed to apologize to Petunia and the piglets. His mouth watered just thinking about the coleslaw, potato salad and baked beans that went with it. Not to mention Gwen's special baked goods.

Ruby stepped out on the front porch and sniffed the air. "Hey, it really smells good. I can't wait to show you off to all my friends," she said, coming down the steps.

"Our friends, Ruby," Sam corrected, squeezing her close. "You know, I used to love the way the 'military family' came together in times of need and happiness, but I've just come to realize that the good folks of Jester are a lot like them."

Ruby nodded. "I thought you'd never figure it out. Just like the 'family' you left, the people in Jester are here for you, to help you through the bad times and to celebrate the good. Why do you think I love it here so much?"

"I think I'm just beginning to figure that out," Sam said. "Now, let's finish getting ready before our guests catch us smooching on the porch."

"Somehow, I don't think they'd bat an eyelash, Sam. They'd probably cheer."

"Hoo-ah!" Sam said. "You got that right."

THE ROCKY GULCH BAND, hired in from Pine Run for the special occasion, struck up a lively tune, and Ruby laughingly pulled Sam into her arms. "Come, husband. We worked all day yesterday to put this dance floor up, and I'll be darned if I'm going to let it go to waste."

"Aw, Ruby, I'm tired from all this getting ready," Sam grumbled good-naturedly as he followed Ruby to the makeshift dance floor. He had spent most of the afternoon yesterday putting the floor together, and Ruby had strung miles of Christmas lights all around to give the space a holiday feel. But he guessed until somebody got the guests started, the dance floor would go to waste.

Ruby was wearing the same red dress she'd had on for their "first date" at the Heartbreaker Saloon, and she looked even better tonight, if that was possible.

Apparently the band had noticed her outfit as well, for they shifted songs suddenly and broke into a country version of "Lady in Red."

Sam looked down into Ruby's laughing face and emerald-green eyes. The slight breeze teased her wavy hair, and tendrils of her coppery locks fluttered around her freckle-dusted face. "Happy, Ruby?" he whispered softly into her ear as Amanda and Dev joined them on the dance floor.

"Ecstatic," Ruby answered. "Now I have almost everything I've ever wanted."

"Almost?"

Ruby started to answer, but a commotion interrupted her reply. "What's going on?"

Sam turned to see a television news truck, complete with microwave dish on top, pull onto the grounds. "Who in the hell invited them?" he grumbled. "Isn't it bad enough that we have that reporter Harvey Brinkman from the *Pine Run Plain Talker* wandering around here, ducking behind the shrubbery and looking like a news bureau chief on a secret mission? The *Plain Talker* is one thing, but television?"

There were several other strangers lurking around the fringes of the party and carrying cameras, as well. Sam figured they were reporters, too.

Ruby chuckled at Sam's description. "Ignore Harvey. He's harmless. And we've gotten so used to having newspeople underfoot around here that we pretty much ignore them unless they stick a microphone under our nose."

"Easy for you to say," Sam said, as a leggy, platinum blonde stepped out of the van. "You're an old pro at it. This is new to me."

Sighing, Ruby craned her neck to see what the reporter was up to. "Well, one of these days, somebody else will get their fifteen minutes of fame, and the attention will shift to them. For now, we just have to grin and bear it."

"Amen to that one."

The reporter flipped through a dog-eared steno pad, then headed toward the dance floor. Behind her lagged a skinny young man carrying a video camera that had to weigh twice as much as he did. Sam muttered a curse. "Hell," he said. "I recognize her. Isn't she on one of those show biz tabloid shows?"

"Yes, she is," Ruby said, frowning. "Funny, I

don't think she's been here before. I wonder what her angle is.''

"I can guess," Sam said sourly. "Reunited lovers, the wounded hero returns…all that smarmy stuff. I think I'm gonna puke." He turned. "I'm going to make myself scarce." He could hold his own in a firefight, if necessary, but the thought of facing that reporter in front of a camera scared him spitless.

"Too late," Ruby said, as the woman, coiffed in a long flip hairdo, the kind that hadn't been seen since the sixties, and clad in a clingy spandex miniskirt and a matching top that showed off her ample bosom to eye-popping advantage, seemed to hone in on them as if she was using a tracking device.

Sam tried not to stare, but he felt like a deer caught in the headlights of a speeding Mack truck as the woman approached. It was too late to make a tactical retreat; she had seen him. He felt as though he were facing a firing squad.

"Smile," Ruby said though gritted teeth. "You're on television."

"I don't feel like smiling," Sam practically growled as the woman and her cameraman planted themselves in front of them.

"Mr. and Mrs. Cade?" the woman asked, though Sam was certain she knew exactly who they were.

Ruby pasted a saccharine smile on her face, the kind she'd always affected when being presented to some general's wife or other dignitary when Sam was on active duty. "I'm Ruby Cade," she said. "And this is my husband, *Captain* Sam Cade."

Sam appreciated the way Ruby had emphasized his military rank, but that seemed a moot point. He was pretty sure the woman—what was her name?—knew

exactly what his rank had been. He stuck out his hand
as a flashbulb exploded in his face. Her handshake
was limp and clammy, and Sam felt as if he were
shaking hands with a dead fish. He swallowed his
distaste and forced a friendly smile. Maybe some people liked the idea of being on television, but as far as
he was concerned, he'd rather have dental surgery.
"I'm Sam Cade. What can I do for you?"

Funny, he thought, the woman was so impressed
with herself that she hadn't even bothered to tell him
her name.

"Well, Sam, Mrs. Cade, I think our viewers would
like to know something about your wonderful love
story and happy reunion."

Behind the woman, and out of the view of the camera, Ruby rolled her eyes. Gwen Tanner looked as
though she were heading toward them, but she turned
quickly and went the other way as another camera
bulb flashed. Sam fervently wished he had been able
to make a getaway as Gwen had.

He took a moment to think. If this was going to be
the line of questioning the reporter intended to pursue,
it was gonna be a damned long night.

RUBY BREATHED A LONG, low sigh of relief as the
reporter—Margaret Sundquist, if she remembered
correctly from watching the show a few times—
strolled away, swinging her ample hips as if everyone's eyes were on her. And they probably were: she
was making such a spectacle of herself.

At least the interview was over with, and so far,
no one else had approached them for another. Harvey
Brinkman, looking cherubic with his curly blond hair
and boyish face, seemed to be content to record the

evening's happenings without talking to her, and that was just fine with Ruby.

"See, that wasn't so bad," she said, slipping her hand into Sam's and squeezing.

"Speak for yourself, woman," he growled. "I'd sooner face a court-martial than have to do that again. I won't rest easy until that woman drives away with all her camera equipment."

"What's this?" Ruby asked, pinching Sam's cheek as a maiden aunt would her favorite nephew. "Big bad ex-combat controller is scared by an itty-bitty television reporter? Who would've thought such a thing?"

Sam growled, a feral sound low in the back of his throat, and turned away. "I have a good mind to get a gun and run all those..." he groped for the right word "...those infernal reporters off." He started toward the house.

"Oh, right," Ruby muttered, catching his arm and pulling him back. "That'll go over like a lead balloon. Just think of the headlines that would make! It would end up in more than just the 'Neighborly Nuggets from Jester' column in the *Plain Talker*. It would make national headlines." She paused. "Besides, I don't have a gun."

"Well, if this keeps up, I'm seriously considering getting one."

"Sam, you have guests here, the reporter is leaving, and everything will be fine. Now go enjoy your party. It is for you, you know!"

"No," Sam said fiercely, drawing Ruby into his arms. "This party is for both of us."

An overwhelming feeling of happiness worked its way through her, and Ruby's heart swelled with joy.

It was so wonderful having Sam back in her life. She felt as if all her hopes and dreams and desires were finally within her reach. Standing here with Sam in her arms, she felt as though everything was right with the world.

"I love you, Sam," she whispered, her voice thick with emotion.

He pulled her closer and pressed a quick kiss to her lips. "You are the best thing that ever happened to me," he said.

Then Mayor Bobby Larson approached, and Ruby and Sam stepped apart. They did have guests to entertain, and even if Bobby Larson wasn't one of her close friends, the man was a guest. Ruby pasted a welcoming smile to her face and reached toward the mayor. "Mayor Larson, I'm so happy you could join us," she said, hoping her insincerity did not show through.

The mayor was sweating profusely in the warm June air. He mopped at his face with a handkerchief, then jammed it in the pocket of his loud plaid slacks and offered his hand to Ruby.

His grip was hot and damp, but at least his handshake was firm, Ruby thought. "Have you met my husband, Sam?"

"Don't believe I've had the pleasure," Bobby said, thrusting his hand toward Sam.

"No, I believe your father was the mayor last time I was here. Congratulations on taking over the job," Sam said, shaking hands, and then looking as though he wanted to dry his fingers on his pant leg.

Bobby rocked back on the heels of his scuffed white bucks, hooked his fingers in the loops of his plaid pants and beamed. "Wonderful party, Ruby.

Thank you for inviting me," he said. "Now, if you don't mind, I have some business to talk to your husband about."

Ruby felt almost as relieved not to have to entertain the mayor as she'd been when the reporter had finally gone on her way. Let Sam deal with Bobby. Besides, she was certain he was going to pester Sam for support for the hotel he wanted to put on the old pavilion site. She made her excuses and hurried away.

Gwen Tanner had apparently been looking for her. And now that the reporter and her truck were definitely gone, Ruby wondered what Gwen had wanted.

"WHAT WAS ALL THAT ABOUT?" Luke McNeil asked as Sam made a hasty retreat from the mayor. Luke was just back from a quick trip to Las Vegas, where he and Jennifer had been married. The surprising news of their elopement had the whole town buzzing.

"As if you don't know," Sam said, striding toward the huge barbecue cooker. The mayor's chat had left him with a bad taste in his mouth, and he thought maybe some barbecue would counteract it.

"Still pushing for the hotel?" Luke followed him to where the remains of the pork were keeping warm on the grill.

"Got that in one," Sam said. "He wanted me to invest. I don't know why, but something about that man makes me uneasy."

"You aren't the only one," Luke said, looking over his shoulder. "He has more than enough motive to have engineered the collapse of the pavilion."

"Why doesn't he just build a hotel on his own property?" Sam asked, loading a paper plate with pork and potatoes. He would have liked a piece of pie to top it all off, but apparently Gwen's delectable desserts were all gone. Unless there were more inside.

Luke piled pork on a bun and ladled a good portion of sauce over it. "Doesn't own any," he said, then took a bite of his sandwich. He chewed and swallowed. "All he's got is a house near the city hall."

"Got it. He has delusions of grandeur without the means to back it up."

"Yeah, and he's been pestering the millionaires to back him ever since they collected their winnings. Even lined up some other investors on the assumption the town would go for the idea. He was dumbfounded that they didn't." Luke reached into a cooler of iced drinks. "I'm never really off duty, but I need this," he said, pulling out a long-neck bottle of beer.

"The mayor is enough to drive a man to drink," Sam said dryly, hooking a beer of his own.

RUBY HAD BEEN SIDETRACKED by Wyla Thorne on her way inside, but fortunately, Wyla hadn't taken up too much of her time. Surprisingly enough, the woman actually thanked her for her invitation to the party. They'd chatted briefly, though Ruby couldn't help wondering if what they'd discussed would wind up in the *Plain Talker*. She'd done her best to keep the conversation trivial, and felt fairly certain she hadn't let slip any deep dark secrets.

Not that she and Sam really had any.

She found Gwen sitting at the kitchen table, looking weary, her head resting on her hand. Gwen smiled tiredly and tried to push herself up out of the chair.

Ruby gestured for her to remain seated, and joined her at the table. "You look tired, Gwen. I don't mind if you head on home." She smiled. "We can eat all these goodies without your help."

Gwen laughed. "I'm sure you can. I was coming out to see you and tell you I was going on home, but I saw that—that reporter had collared you and Sam, so I came back inside."

"Good move," Ruby said. Gwen might be prepared to raise her children alone, but Ruby was sure she had no desire to have her pregnant condition displayed on national television.

"Yes, it was good that I came back inside," Gwen said. "Sam had a phone call. I took a message." She leaned back in her chair, grimaced and pressed her hand against her huge belly. "One or both of the babies are kicking," she said by way of explanation. "I had no idea such little creatures could kick so hard."

"Well, it won't be long now," Ruby said.

"No, just a couple of months, and the doctor says that twins often come early." She sighed wearily. "I hope so, just not too early. Though I would like to be able to see my feet again," she said with a wry smile.

Ruby looked down. "They are quite lovely feet, just like the rest of you. There's something quite beautiful about a pregnant woman, you know," she said wistfully. How she'd hoped to someday find herself in the same condition.

"You only say that because you're not getting up every hour on the hour in the middle of the night to go to the bathroom. Just wait," Gwen said. "I don't know if I'll ever have enough sleep again." She pushed herself up and adjusted her jumper over her belly. "I hope you don't mind, but I really want to go home now. Has that reporter gone? Is the coast clear?''

''As far as I know it is,'' Ruby said, getting up, too. ''Of course I don't mind if you go home, Gwen. You need your rest.''

Gwen looked around for her purse. ''Thank you for inviting me,'' she said, and started for the door.

''Bye, Gwen,'' Ruby said, then watched her friend lumber away.

Then her gaze rested on the telephone on the wall. ''Oh. What about the phone message?''

Gwen looked over her shoulder. ''I wrote it down on the message board. It was for Sam.''

Ruby smiled. ''Thanks, Gwen. I'll pass it on to him.''

Then she looked at the message scrawled on the board.

''Call Cap,'' Gwen had written. Below it was a number. The rest of the message read, ''It's a done deal.''

''Oh, God,'' Ruby murmured, sinking back into the chair she'd just vacated. Not after all this time. ''Why now?'' she wailed. She'd always liked Cap, but she'd never liked his schemes. Sam had.

If she told him about the phone call, Ruby was convinced that Sam wouldn't hesitate to accept.

She was caught on the horns of a dilemma. If she simply erased the message off the board, it would be as if the phone call had never happened. Sam would never know. But then Ruby remembered Cap's persistence. He would call back.

He would pester Sam until he accepted. And Sam would be off again, flying into danger. And she'd be home worrying as she always had.

Even if she didn't tell Sam, and Cap accepted Sam's failure to call him back as disinterest, she would know. It would worry at her conscience until she had to tell Sam.

She wondered how long it would take her husband to accept the offered opportunity for more excitement than he would find in slow, sleepy Jester, Montana.

Just when Ruby had thought that she and Sam had finally worked through most of their problems, Cap had to call. Now they were all the way back to square one. Ruby wanted to kick or throw something. It wouldn't accomplish much, but there was something satisfying about hearing a nice, solid thump, or the sound of something crashing to the ground. But she didn't. She had company to tend to, though she'd lost any semblance of a festive mood.

She pasted on a fake smile and hurried back outside to her guests.

Chapter Sixteen

Sam was waylaid at least three times on his way back to the house by guests thanking him for the invitation and making their excuses to leave. If he weren't in such a hurry to find Ruby, he'd have enjoyed the short chats, but a familiar, odd feeling in his gut told him that something was wrong. He'd learned to trust that feeling in action, and he'd trust it now. There was no way Ruby would be hiding inside when she had guests to entertain if everything were okay.

Gwen came out of the house, looking tired and ready to go home. Sam stopped to help her settle her bulky form into her car, then directed traffic to allow her to get out onto the lane ahead of the other vehicles. He'd been careful about how much alcohol any one party guest had consumed, but he also knew that Gwen was exhausted, and he wanted to make sure she made it home safely before the rest of the guests crowded the roads.

He stood and watched as her car bumped down the lane, and hoped that the rutty conditions would not hurry her into premature labor. Not that he knew very much about those sorts of things. Once he saw

Gwen's headlights turn onto the paved main road, Sam relaxed.

He turned toward the newly painted house, hoping that no one would stop him this time.

Feeling like a kid who'd broken curfew and was dreading the consequences, he hurried inside.

Ruby was slumped over the kitchen table, her face pale, her green eyes downcast, looking as if she'd lost her last friend. Certainly not the right attitude for a woman who'd recently reconciled with her husband and was throwing a party to celebrate.

He rushed to her and took her hands in his. They were cold, adding to his feeling of unease. "What's wrong, Ruby? Have you had some bad news?"

Ruby shook her head as if she hadn't realized he was there. She blinked a couple of times and seemed to focus. "No, nothing's wrong. I'm just tired," she said, not sounding very convincing to a man whose gut was telling him a different story.

"Then why are you sitting here alone in the kitchen?" Sam tried not to sound threatening, but something was bothering Ruby, and he had every intention of getting to the bottom of it.

Vaguely waving toward the wall phone behind her, Ruby answered, her tone still listless, "You had a phone call. Gwen took the message."

There, scrawled on the chalk board, was a note that his best air force buddy had called. "Cap called? When?"

Ruby shrugged. "Gwen took the message," she said. "I wasn't here. I think it was when we were being interviewed by the blonde from the television show."

Sam glanced at his watch. He'd love to talk to Cap,

but it was late, and it was two time zones later where Cap was. "I'll call him tomorrow. I'd like to hear what he has going for him."

That was exactly what Ruby did not want to hear. The only thing that would have eased her mind would have been for Sam to tell her completely and definitively that he did not want to take that job. Not now. Not ever. Her hopes plummeted. It sounded as if he might actually be considering it.

Ruby had thought she'd made her feelings about Sam being in danger perfectly clear when he'd taken that assignment overseas. If she hadn't then, surely she'd made her point by filing for divorce.

Now she wasn't at all sure Sam cared.

"The guests are starting to leave," he said, interrupting her train of thought. "We should go out and say goodbye. Then I have to see to it that everything is put away."

"Yeah, you go," Ruby said, not really caring about her guests at this moment. "I'll see to putting the baked goods away in here."

There was no way Ruby could muster up anything that came close to a festive mood, so she continued to hide out in the kitchen. She busied herself arranging the few remaining pastries from the party platters onto one. Anything to keep from looking at Sam.

Ruby was afraid if she did, she'd give her feelings away. And one thing she did not want to do was influence Sam's final decision about Cap's job offer in any way. She would only be certain that Sam truly wanted to be with her if he made his decision on his own.

The screen door slammed, telling her that Sam had gone out, and Ruby felt free to let her feelings go.

Maybe if she got it out of her system now, she'd be able to face Sam later without him suspecting. She felt the sting of unshed tears, and tried to blink them back.

"Ruby? Is something wrong?"

She looked up to see that Honor had come in just as Sam went out. Ruby swallowed and turned away. "No, I'm okay," she lied, her voice strangely thick and gravelly.

"You are not. I've known you for most of our lives, and there's no way you can make me believe you're all right," Honor said, sitting down next to Ruby. "Look at me."

"No," she said stubbornly. She squeezed her eyes shut, but it was becoming increasingly difficult to hold back the impending flood.

Honor took her hand and tugged it, forcing Ruby to look at her. "Something is wrong, my friend. Tell me about it. You know you'll feel better. Is it something about your mom in Denver?"

Ruby shook her head. "No, Mom's fine. The heart doctor said that if she stays on her diet and continues to exercise there's no reason for her not to live a long and healthy life." As much as she tried to keep her voice calm and level, a sob escaped at the end of her little speech. "Oh, Honor, I don't know what to do."

"About what, honey?" Honor said, flipping her long blond hair over her shoulders. She took both of Ruby's hands in hers and looked deep into her eyes.

"One of Sam's military buddies has invited him to go into business with him," Ruby wailed, no longer trying to choke back her tears.

"But that's good, isn't it?"

"No, Cap was always talking about setting up a

bodyguard service. And Sam was always right there with him making those plans.'' She picked up one of the paper party napkins remaining on the table and studied the pattern intensely.

"Oh, Ruby," Honor said. "And you're afraid Sam's going to take his friend up on his offer and leave again?"

Tears coursing down her face, Ruby nodded numbly.

"Has he said he would?"

Ruby shook her head. "He said he'd call Cap back in the morning. I can't bear the thought of more years of sitting at home alone and worrying about him like I did before. Not now."

"But he didn't say he would accept it, Ruby."

"He didn't say he wouldn't."

Honor squeezed Ruby's hands. "You have to ask him about it."

"I can't," Ruby said again, stopping to swipe at the tears that were blurring her eyes. And probably her thinking, too.

"Sure you can. You've been married to Sam for ten years. You two can talk about anything."

"Not about this," Ruby insisted. "I don't want to influence him. I need to be sure he really wants to be here with me."

"Why wouldn't you be certain? It's plain as the nose on your face that he loves you."

"Is it? It's not to me," Ruby whispered, a litany of unvoiced doubts coming into her mind.

"Oh, come on, Ruby," Honor said, her gray eyes as cloudy as Ruby's surely were. "Anybody who looks at him can see it. Why, I'd give anything to have a man look at me the way Sam looks at you.

What makes you think he isn't head over heels in love with you? My goodness, Ruby. The man practically camped out on your porch till you took him back. I never saw a guy as determined as he was,'' Honor added.

''Then why hasn't he brought home all his belongings?'' She twisted the napkin in her fingers.

''He hasn't? I saw him load his car up with his things from the apartment.''

''I mean the rest of his stuff—the stuff in storage that he took with him overseas. All he brought with him to Jester were the bare necessities, not much more than would fill an overnight bag.'' Ruby let go of the twisted napkin and watched as it relaxed and unrolled. If only she could relax. ''Why would he leave his possessions in storage unless he thought he'd need to make a fast getaway? When I asked him why he didn't have more, he said he was waiting until he was sure.''

''He could have meant that he wanted to be sure you still wanted him,'' Honor suggested quietly.

Ruby shook her head. ''No, it's what he didn't say. Three little words.'' She looked down at the shredded mess that was once a party napkin. ''All this time he's been saying he wanted me back, but he's never said he loves me. Not once. I can't help wondering if it's more a matter of male pride and ownership than love,'' she murmured, voicing the nagging doubts that had been lying so close to the surface since Sam had come back to Jester. ''You know how men hate to lose at anything.''

Honor gathered Ruby into her arms for a tight bear hug. ''Oh, Ruby, I don't think it's anything like that.

Sam loves you. I'd bet my half of the Mercantile on it."

Ruby pushed herself out of her friend's embrace and managed a watery smile. "I hope you're right," she said. "Though I'd hate to relieve you of your livelihood," she added with a feeble chuckle.

Honor waved dismissively. "I'm not worried. I've got a million bucks I can live on."

"Well, why doesn't he say it, then?"

Honor pushed herself up out of the chair. "Considering I'm the oldest living virgin in Jester, I'm the last one to give you advice for the lovelorn, but I've read enough books to know a thing or two about men. In theory, anyway. And they're not talkers. If you want to know if Sam loves you, you might have to ask him."

"I can't. It has to come spontaneously from him, or I'm not sure I'll believe it."

"Believe me, Ruby. That man loves you."

"I don't know, Honor. I just have to wait and see what he does about Cap's plan. If he doesn't take the job, maybe then I'll ask him." Ruby pushed herself to her feet and began to fiddle with the cookies, rearranging them on their plates.

"If he doesn't take the job, Ruby," Honor said quietly, "then you won't have to ask him."

Ruby wiped her eyes on another party napkin and sniffed back one last tear. "You're probably right. I guess I can hang on a little longer."

"Believe me, kiddo. By tomorrow, you'll know for sure."

Ruby pasted an anemic smile on her face. "From your lips to God's ears," she said. Now, if she could only survive until tomorrow.

SAM STOOD OUTSIDE and directed the stream of friends, neighbors and guests out toward the highway. All the while, he silently worried about why Ruby wasn't there with them to see their guests off. It wasn't like her. Not at all.

He watched as the Rocky Gulch Band packed up their instruments and drove away. When the last car had pulled out of the driveway and its red taillights had disappeared into the darkness, he silently blew out the tiki torches, then disconnected the lights over the makeshift dance floor.

Alone in the night, illuminated only by the security lamp and the lights from the house, Sam drew in a deep breath of fresh air, tinged slightly with the scent of hickory smoked barbecue, and sighed with satisfaction. All in all, he'd have to say it had been one hell of a good party. Until the last few minutes, anyway.

Ruby had been the consummate hostess up until then, and no one could have looked more beautiful than his lady in red. Of course, there would be plenty of work to do tomorrow to get everything cleaned up, but it had certainly been worth it.

No man could have shown his friends and neighbors any better how much he loved and adored his wife and how happy he was with his newfound life.

If anyone had ever told him, back when he was on active duty, that he'd love being a farmer, he would have laughed him out of the room. But now he realized he really did like the slower, easy pace of life. And it didn't hurt that he and Ruby had money and the Mercantile to fall back on.

Sam took another deep breath of night air. Yeah,

he was gonna love growing old with Ruby. It might be damned cold out here in Montana in the winters, but with her there to snuggle up with and keep him warm, he'd learn to love the ice and snow as much as he loved her.

The lights blinked off in the kitchen behind him, reminding Sam just how late it really was. It was well after midnight, and now that he stopped to think about it, he realized he was dead tired. He stowed what stuff he figured stood a chance of blowing away and decided the rest could wait until morning.

For now, the most important thing was getting his tired body to bed.

With Ruby.

MAYBE IT WAS COWARDLY of her, but Ruby was in no mood to talk to Sam tonight, much less make love. She'd rushed through straightening up the kitchen and her evening beauty ritual, and made certain that she was in bed with the lights off before Sam came inside. She might lie awake all night, but she would do anything to make him think she was sound asleep.

Morning would come soon enough. And then she'd know how Sam felt.

Once and for all.

She lay there in the concealing darkness, covers pulled up to her chin in spite of the summer warmth, and listened to the sounds of the night. A gentle breeze rustled the leaves of the cottonwood tree outside the open window, and the old house creaked and groaned as it settled down for the night.

She listened as Sam came inside, locked the doors and made his nightly rounds, checking window locks, turning off the rest of the lights. Slowly the sounds of his footsteps came nearer, and Ruby tensed.

Surely he was as tired as she. But what would she do if he wanted to talk? Or to make love?

How would she conceal her true feelings? How would she be able to keep from begging him to stay?

No, she told herself as she squeezed her eyes tightly shut. It was late, and she was unusually tired. She would not think about that. She needed this one last night to fortify herself for what might come.

Sam's footsteps came down the hall, and Ruby watched him walk past, his shadow momentarily blacking out the light sliding under the door from the hall. She heard the sound of water running and all the other normal bedtime sounds that had become so familiar as she'd become accustomed to having Sam home again. Then the hall light blinked out, extinguishing that feeble bit of illumination.

The door swung quietly open and Sam tiptoed in. "Ruby, are you asleep?"

She said nothing, and he must have taken her silence as an answer. The mattress dipped and creaked with his weight, and Ruby listened as he removed his shoes and peeled off his socks. She recognized the rustling sound as he removed his Western shirt, worn especially for the festive occasion, and then the distinctive sound of his zipper sliding down. The bed dipped and rocked and shook as he slowly removed his clothes.

Then he lifted the covers, letting in a rush of cool air, and slid under them.

Ruby thought that would be it, and that Sam would settle down to sleep. But what he did next surprised her. She felt Sam lean over her, brush her hair away from her cheek and gently kiss her, and she pushed aside a momentary desire to roll over and return the kiss. Then, with a satisfied sigh, Sam rolled back to his territory on the mattress.

She felt the rustle of the covers as he plumped his pillow and made himself comfortable on his side of the bed, settling in like an old friendly dog on a rug in front of the fire. Finally, the shaky movement of the mattress came to an end, and Ruby realized she was feeling vaguely queasy.

Breathing in the familiar, tantalizing fragrance of Sam's aftershave, Ruby was surprised that it was still faintly recognizable this late in the evening. She pushed back a wave of desire, swallowed and rolled carefully to her side. She hugged her pillow and clung to the edge of the mattress. Now she just had to make it through the rest of the night.

Suddenly, she felt Sam's hand settle possessively on her hip. She felt the heat of desire in his touch as he seemed to brand her, as if to prove she belonged to him. She stifled a small gasp, but concealed it with a subtle shift of position. She'd hoped to dislodge the hand, but she couldn't brush it away, and Sam continued to hold her, to own her.

She wished she could feel as confident about Sam as he apparently did about her.

In spite of her nagging insecurity, Ruby liked the feeling of his hand against her body, loved the feeling of connection and oneness it brought. If only that unspoken link would continue forever. She hadn't expected to be able to sleep a wink, but with Sam's comforting presence, Ruby settled into a deep sleep, in spite of her mental turmoil.

SAM WOKE FEELING RESTED and refreshed and ready to start his day. He yawned and stretched, then slid out of bed.

Ruby was still sleeping, and he hadn't the heart to wake her. She'd been as busy as he'd been preparing for the party, so she deserved a few extra winks. Maybe he could surprise her with breakfast in bed.

He tiptoed through the quiet house to the kitchen and started the coffee, forgotten last night in all the excitement of the party. Then he turned back to the bathroom, where he took his morning shower. Maybe by the time he was finished, Ruby would be up. Or maybe she'd join him.

She didn't.

Still, Sam was willing to let her sleep. Ruby had seemed bothered by something last night, and there was plenty of time for her to work on the farm later. It sure wasn't going anywhere.

With a cup of freshly brewed coffee and one of Gwen's delectable pastries, he settled down, phone in hand, to call Cap. Sam took a sip of coffee, a bite of pastry, and chewed thoughtfully before he dialed. He knew Cap was anxious for an answer, and Sam had one for him. His friend wouldn't like his terms, but there was only one way he would buy into the scheme. Thus fortified, Sam dialed the long distance number.

Cap could take it or leave it.

IT WAS TOO FAR from the kitchen for Ruby to hear what Sam was saying on the telephone, but she knew he'd made the call. Maybe it was cowardly of her, but she couldn't bring herself to get out of bed to find out once and for all. As long as she didn't know, she still had hope. As long as Sam didn't tell her, she could pretend to believe, no matter how unreasonably, that he would do the right thing.

As long as she didn't ask.

Suddenly cold, in spite of the warm June morning, she pulled the covers more tightly around her. Today could be the turning point in her life with Sam, or without him. But the good news was that soon she'd have an answer, one way or the other. In the meantime, Ruby was in no hurry to rush it.

What would be would be.

It was out of her hands.

Sam called from the kitchen. "Hey, I've got bacon cooking. Are you up for eggs? Or I could make French toast."

Ruby's tense stomach turned at the thought of bacon and eggs, but she swallowed her discomfort long enough to answer. "Just juice and toast for me," she called, her voice sounding feeble. But maybe it was just because she was buried so deeply in her covers. "I think I had too much to eat at the party last night."

"Are you coming, then?"

Ruby threw the covers aside and gingerly levered her legs over the edge of the mattress. "Yes, I'm up." Her stomach was quite unsettled this morning. More than unsettled. Her stressed out situation was apparently making her downright sick.

She stumbled to the bathroom and showered, forcing herself awake. She hadn't stayed up that late last night, and she hadn't had a thing to drink. Nothing alcoholic, anyway. Why did she feel as though she were hungover?

She stayed in the shower until the water ran luke-warm, but still didn't feel thoroughly herself. Fumbling into her clothes, she made her way slowly out to the kitchen.

Just as she reached the kitchen door, the phone rang. Ruby didn't know whether it was the sound of the phone or the smell of the bacon, but her stomach lurched, and she clung to the doorjamb to hold herself up.

Sam hadn't seen her. He stood there looking as though he didn't have a care in the world as he listened to the person who had called. His dear, handsome face widened with a grin.

Was Cap Horton on the other end of the line? Had he called back to try again to make Sam an offer he couldn't resist?

"Hoo-ah!" she heard Sam cheer. "I'm on the way." Then he hung up the phone and turned for the door, still not noticing Ruby.

He must have remembered that he'd offered her breakfast, for when he was about to step outside the mudroom, he shouted over his shoulder, "Ruby, I've got something to take care of in town. I'll be back later to tell you all the details about Cap's offer." Then he was gone.

Though Sam had said he'd be back, Ruby couldn't help wondering if this was the beginning of the end. She closed her eyes, hoping to dredge up some minute bit of strength, and drew in a deep breath. The smell of bacon and coffee slammed into her like a sledgehammer, and she turned and ran to the bathroom.

And promptly threw up.

Chapter Seventeen

Sam grinned as he pocketed a wad of cash big enough to choke his billfold and then shook hands with Tex Youngblood. "Good doing business with you, man," he said, slapping the grizzled garage mechanic on the back.

"Any time you want to come back and visit, you're welcome to," Tex said, wiping his greasy hands on a rag only marginally cleaner than he was.

"Thanks for the offer, Tex, but I've had my fill of her. I got something that works better for me now."

Still pleased with the bargain he'd made, Sam headed out to the parking lot.

"Yup," he told himself as he started the powerful engine of his new truck. "This is gonna be the start of something big. The sky's the limit." He rolled down the window and let out a triumphant yell. "Hoo-ah!" he cheered. "This is gonna be the first day of the rest of my life."

Then he gunned the engine and headed for the road.

RUBY FINALLY PULLED herself together, dressed and managed to choke down some dry toast and orange juice. She still felt awful, but she didn't think she'd throw up again. The last thing she needed right now was to find out she'd poisoned all her friends and neighbors with something she'd served last night. Instead, she just hoped it was a simple case of nerves.

Something rattled the mudroom screen door, and Ruby looked out to see Oscar pawing at the door as if he were trying to come inside.

"What's the matter, little piggy? Are you hungry and nobody's come out to feed you?" She forced a smile, not that Oscar would probably notice it, as she made her way outside. It was amazing to her how much like a dog Oscar seemed. Or like a child. A child that might grow up to weigh hundreds of pounds.

She stepped outside, the bright morning sun causing her red, irritated eyes to sting and burn. She squinted, but didn't stop to find her hat or sunglasses. A few minutes out in the sun wouldn't hurt her, one way or another. Not compared to the constant ache in the space where her heart should be.

Oscar snorted urgently, and Ruby picked up her pace toward the hog shed. "Okay, babe. I'll feed you and the family."

Surely Sam would have taken care of the pigs, she thought. But maybe he was feeling as ill as she was. Then she remembered. He'd gone to town.

The piglet trotted behind her, his little hooves beating a merry tattoo behind her. At least somebody was in a good mood today, Ruby couldn't help thinking. She wasn't sure she ever would be again.

As they approached the hog pen, Petunia, with Oscar's littermates, scampered to the fence. They lined up along the fence rails, expectantly waiting to be fed. Petunia voiced her indignance at being kept waiting, and the others picked up her complaint in a chorus of petulant oinks.

"I'm coming. I'm coming," Ruby said, feeling suddenly peeved and harassed. "Three months ago your mother was out there in the woods foraging for food, and now you complain about being fed an hour late?" she grumbled, not expecting an answer.

"Okay, smarty pig," she said. "Maybe if I give you an extra ration of food you'll grow big enough not to keep slipping under the fence."

She turned, went into the shed and scooped up a bucketful of dry hog chow. "You know," she told Oscar as she poured the food into the trough, "I sort of enjoy having you trot around after me right now, but one day you will be an adult hog. Maybe I should get a dog."

Oscar gave her a wounded look, then turned his attention to the trough and the chow, gobbling it down with a grunting chorus of approval.

Something told her to look up, and Ruby glanced toward the road, to where a huge black truck she didn't recognize was bumping toward her, sending up a dusty plume behind it.

She shaded her eyes and watched it as it approached. Ruby just hoped it wasn't somebody coming from the county health department because her barbecue had made half the population of Jester sick.

Finally the big black truck pulled up in front of the hog shed. Ruby tried to see who was inside, but she could make out nothing more than a shadow through the tinted windshield.

Then a familiar figure stepped out of the cab and waved.

Suddenly Ruby's world seemed right again. "Sam!"

she called, half surprised, half elated. She ran forward and rushed into his arms. "Where did you get this enormous truck? Where's the Corvette?" she demanded from the shelter of his arms.

"Hey, sweetness. One question at a time," Sam said, crushing her in a bear hug and kissing the top of her head. "I ordered the truck a couple of weeks ago. The Corvette just wasn't working out that well as a farm car. Got the call it was in at the dealership in Pine Run this morning."

"That's where you rushed off to this morning? To pick up the truck? What did you do with your car? You loved the Corvette."

"Tex has been pestering me to buy it ever since I started garaging it with him between my leaves from duty. I finally let him have her." He paused and patted his hip pocket. "Well, I didn't exactly give it to him. He drove a hard bargain, but we made out all right," he said, grinning and patting his pocket again. "And he said I could come visit her anytime I felt lonely for her."

"Why didn't you tell me?"

"I wanted to surprise you," Sam said, setting her back out of his arms. "Can't a guy get just a little bit of pleasure from surprising the lady he loves now and then? Come. Look."

Ruby started to let Sam show her the truck, then stopped stock-still in the middle of the farmyard. "What did you say?"

Sam looked at her, his gray eyes puzzled. "About what? I said, come look."

"No, before that."

He shook his head, his eyes narrowed, his brow furrowed, obviously still puzzled.

"The *L* word. Did you really mean it?"

Suddenly, what Ruby was asking seemed to dawn on Sam, judging by the look on his face. "That I love you? Didn't you know that already? Hell, I came back for you." He yanked Ruby into his arms.

"I thought so," she said. "That's why we had the party. But after that phone call last night, I wasn't sure you'd be content to stay here."

"What? Cap's business proposition? I took him up on it."

Ruby's heart ceased to beat. "You what?" She pushed herself out of Sam's arms and stared up into his dark gray eyes.

How could he do that to her? How could he make her so happy one minute and then disappoint her so much a moment later?

"I agreed to be a partner in Horton Security," he said. "A silent partner. I figure I'll front some of the money and let Cap do all the work." He shrugged. "Maybe he'll make a go of it, maybe he won't. But we go back a long way. I couldn't turn him down."

Her heart kicked back into rhythm, and Ruby drew a deep breath. "You mean you're not going to leave me here while you go off and…"

"Fight the bad guys?" Sam's eyes narrowed. "Why would I do that when I've got you and the pigs and, maybe one day, a houseful of little Cades to play with?"

Ruby's heart swelled with joy. "You really mean it? You want to stay here for the rest of your life and farm and start a family with me?"

"Of course I do! I've got the most beautiful wife in the world. You've waited for me to settle down long enough. It's time now. I feel it.'' Sam reached for her and drew her back into his arms.

"Then why didn't you bring all your stuff home?"

"What stuff?"

"Your belongings. You didn't bring anything but what you could put in a suitcase.''

"I told you already. I wanted to be sure you'd let me stay. It would have killed me to have to pack up and leave you again.''

"Oh, Sam. I've waited forever to hear you say that.''

"Ruby Albright Cade, don't you know that you are the most precious thing to me? Our marriage is priceless. I swore I'd move heaven and earth to get you to let me come back.''

"And I thought you were just waiting for another, better offer.''

"Sugar, spending the rest of my life with you is the best offer any man could have.''

Sam scooped her up into his arms. "Say, let's go inside and rest up after our exciting night,'' he said, wagging his eyebrows suggestively. "Maybe we can get started on that baby thing.''

Ruby smiled, pressing her face against Sam's broad, strong chest, feeling his heart beating steadily against her cheek. Suddenly her queasiness made sense. "I certainly don't mind going inside with you, Sam,'' she whispered, a little awestruck at her realization. "But you're a little late with that particular proposition. I've been queasy all morning.''

He stopped, seeming not to understand. Then his eyes lit up with realization. "You mean—? We're gonna—?''

Ruby nodded. "I haven't seen Dr. Perkins yet, but

I think so,'' she said, smiling up into Sam's eyes. ''But it wouldn't hurt to keep trying just in case it's a false alarm,'' she said, feeling her eyes fill with tears of happiness.

''Hoo-ah!'' Sam cheered, and he turned toward the house. ''Got that in one. Let's go. I can't wait to get started on the rest of our lives together!''

Ruby just smiled, her head resting against the chest of the man she loved. And who loved her!

As far as she was concerned, they already had started the rest of their lives. But then, she thought, with a baby on the way, the best was yet to come.

* * * * *

Don't miss
FORTUNE'S TWINS
by Kara Lennox,
the exciting, final installment of
MILLIONAIRE, MONTANA.
Available in June 2003,
only from Harlequin American Romance.

HARLEQUIN®

AMERICAN *Romance*®

celebrates its 20th Anniversary

This June, we have a distinctive lineup that features
another wonderful title in

The Deveraux Legacy

series from bestselling author

CATHY GILLEN THACKER

Taking Over the Tycoon
(HAR #973)

Sexy millionaire Connor Templeton is used to
getting whatever—whomever—he wants!
But has he finally met his match in
one beguiling single mother?

And on sale in July 2003,
Harlequin American Romance premieres
a brand-new miniseries,
Cowboys by the Dozen,
from **Tina Leonard.**

Available at your favorite retail outlet.

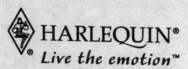

HARLEQUIN®
Live the emotion™

Visit us at www.eHarlequin.com

HAR20CGT

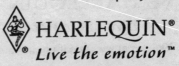

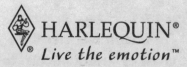

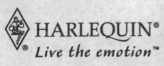

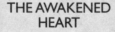

AMERICAN *Romance®*

The Hartwell Hope Chests

RITA HERRON

returns with her heartwarming series.

Something old, something new, something borrowed, something blue. Inside each Hartwell hope chest is a dream come true!

Sisters Rebecca and Suzanne are as different as night and day, but they have one thing in common: a hope chest from Grammy Rose is certain to have them hearing wedding bells!

Have Bouquet, Need Boyfriend
On sale June 2003

Have Cowboy, Need Cupid
On sale July 2003

Available at your favorite retail outlet.

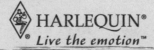

HARLEQUIN®
Live the emotion™

Visit us at www.eHarlequin.com

HARTHHC